The Book of the
Duke of True Lovers

Other books by Christine de Pizan published by Persea

The Book of the City of Ladies
   Translated, with an introduction by Earl Jeffrey Richards
   Foreword by Marina Warner

A Medieval Woman's Mirror of Honor: The Treasury of the City of Ladies
   Translated, with an introduction by Charity Cannon Willard
   Edited, with an introduction by Madeleine Pelner Cosman

The Book of the
Duke of True Lovers

Christine de Pizan

Pisan

Translated, with an introduction
by Thelma S. Fenster

With lyric poetry translated
by Nadia Margolis

Persea Books
New York

For information, write to the publisher:

Persea Books, Inc.
60 Madison Avenue
New York, New York 10010

Library of Congress Cataloging-in-Publication Data

Christine, de Pisan, ca. 1364–ca. 1431.
    [Livre du duc des vrais amants. English].
    The book of the duke of true lovers / Christine de Pizan; translated,
with an introduction by Thelma S. Fenster, with lyric poetry translated
by Nadia Margolis. — 1st ed.
        p.   cm.
    Translation of: Le livre du duc des vrais amants.
    Includes bibliographical references (p. 155).
    ISBN 0-89255-163-1 (cloth)
    ISBN 0-89255-166-6 (pbk.)
    I. Margolis, Nadia, 1949–   II. Title.
PQ1575.L7513   1991
841'.2—dc20   91-31266
                                                        CIP

Designed by Peter St. John Ginna

Typeset in Garamond by Keystrokes, Lenox, Massachusetts
Printed and bound by Haddon Craftsmen, Scranton, Pennsylvania

First Edition

Contents

Illustrations

All illustrations are from Christine de Pizan's collected works, Harley manuscript 4431, and are copyrighted and courtesy of The British Library, London.

Preface

When the "Duke of True Lovers" asked the well-known writer, Christine de Pizan (1365–1430?), to record his tale of love, he probably knew her as the author of courtly lyric poetry, mostly on love themes, and of courtly narrative pieces dealing with love questions: *The Debate of Two Lovers, The Tale of Poissy,* and *The Book of the Three Judgments,* dating from c. 1400. He may also have known her more serious side—the side that would soon gain the ascendant—through the other writing she had done by 1403–05, the span of time within which *The Book of the Duke of True Lovers* was most likely composed: the mythographic *Epistle of Othea to Hector* (1399–1400), the didactic *Book of the Road of Long Learning* (1402–03), her vast moralizing history, *The Mutation of Fortune* (1403), whose modern edition occupies four volumes, and perhaps, her moral treatise, *The Book of Human Integrity* (1403–04), and her *Book of the Deeds and Good Customs of the Wise King Charles V* (1404). But, although Christine had expressed some of her views about women in *The Letter of the God of Love* (1399) and *Tale of the Rose* (1402), and in the debate over *The Romance of the Rose* (1401–1404), she had not yet written *The Book of the Three Virtues* (or *Treasury of the City of Ladies*), and she had probably not yet written *The Book of the City of Ladies,* the two long prose treatises that represent her most substantive statements about women and women's lives.

The Duke may well have expected, therefore, that Christine would be sympathetic to his plight. And she was—but not as completely as he might have hoped. If indeed she had adopted a neutral position about adulterous, courtly love in the three poems written in 1400, by the time of the *Duke of True Lovers,* with her reputation more firmly established, and now being asked once more to write on a subject that held little interest for her, Christine was no longer willing to remain entirely silent. Thus the Duke's imposed story, which Christine nevertheless rendered with great tact, became a vehicle unique in the medieval period: the answer of a flesh-and-blood medieval woman to a literary model that was invoked to justify real-life behavior, one that Christine saw as utterly ruinous for women.

It is a further index of Christine's talent in *The Book of the Duke of True Lovers* and in others of her poems that she could enfold a serious message inside literary creations of great charm. Working at a time when manuscript culture had long since replaced purely oral recitation, she nevertheless had a keen sense of narrative as performance: in this work intrigue joins visual evocation and the sound of many voices to offer a medieval social tableau that would have appealed to her readers as much as it does to modern ones. A version of aristocratic medieval life is represented enticingly in the tournament description, for example, with its attendant feasting and dancing; woven through is the secret love-drama of the Duke and his Lady, played out against a backdrop of public spectacle. Equally of interest are the complex, duplicitous arrangements the Lady devises so that the lovers may be together: the evocation of a great castle whose interior halls and corridors form the clandestine route the Duke and Lady must follow in order to meet in private. These parallel the fateful paths of a countryside in which the Duke, hungering for a passionate love, had first gone hunting and come upon the Lady, and through which messengers carry secret letters between the separated lovers.

The Book of the Duke of True Lovers is among the very best of Christine's longer courtly poems, a lively hybrid work whose color and lyricism alone reward even the most casual reading. In the end, though, the performance serves Christine's intent: to bypass simple *narration* and arrive at the immediacy and point of *demonstration*. In Christine's writing, method and message are rarely far apart.

T.F.

Acknowledgments

Thelma Fenster translated *The Book of the Duke of True Lovers* (the narrative and letters) and prepared the glossary and introduction. Nadia Margolis translated the lyric poetry (the poems inserted into the narrative and those following the end of the Duke's story). In addition, each of us acted as reader for the other's translation.

For help in rendering certain cultural aspects of the translation, Thelma Fenster would like to thank Professors Liliane Dulac, Jean-Michel Mehl, and Charity Cannon Willard, and her student, Laïla Lachani. Fordham University granted her a Faculty Fellowship for one semester, in part for work on this translation. William Dunkle and John Stegeman of the Woods Hole Oceanographic Institution kindly provided equipment and assistance.

Introduction

*T*he Book of the Duke of True Lovers is Christine de Pizan's complex tale of a love affair between the young Duke of the title and a Lady who is his beautiful, but married, cousin. The Duke has asked Christine to tell his story, and though she is reluctant— other pursuits are of more interest to her—she agrees, out of respect for the Duke's station.[1]

For most of this narrative poem of just over 3500 lines, Christine silences her own voice. Instead, the lovers' voices, given free rein, contribute to the poem's polyphonous texture: the courtly lyric poetry (ballade, rondeau, and virelai) in which the young Duke expresses his desire; the lovers' dialogue in miniature that frames the moment of their first secret tryst—when "love becomes dialogue"[2]; and, the prose of their epistolary exchange, employed for the preliminaries of formal declaration. But eventually the lovers' speech is interrupted by the contrasting, urgent prose of Sebille de Monthault, Dame de la Tour, the Lady's former governess: Sebille's older woman's wisdom unfolds in the Latinate, learned-sounding periodic constructions of a long admonitory letter that she writes to the Lady, counseling her to end the liaison. The Dame de la Tour attends to a different group of voices, this one more muffled: it is the offstage murmur of gossiping tongues slowly consolidating themselves into a chaotic force, a whisper of scandal the Lady in particular must fear. With that social concern in mind, Christine fashions the received material, the Duke's story, into a cautionary tale whose concern is, far more palpably, the Lady.[3] In addition, once the Dame de la Tour's moral treatise intrudes upon the courtly romance, *The Book of the Duke of True Lovers* becomes Christine's explicitly anti-courtly courtly romance.

Composed probably between 1403–05, the *Duke of True Lovers* describes a furtive liaison conducted over a period of twelve or thirteen years.[4] Though the inception of the affair is depicted through phases of delicious anticipation, great joy and magnificent spectacle, and the two years after that were relatively happy ones, the curious and the envious soon began to whisper that the Duke was *recreant*—a coward—because he remained in the vicinity, participating only in local tournaments. The Lady's honor was also gravely damaged by the talk about her. To prove himself, and to try to restore some of the Lady's compromised reputation, the Duke must go off to war. He returns whenever possible, endeavoring to see his Lady, but their frequent separations cause both to feel jealousy and suspicion. The poem ends without resolving the lovers' dilemma; that lack of closure emphasizes the impossibility of their love, with its many irreconcilables. The coda of lyric poems that follows the Duke's tale records the suffering of the Duke and Lady in alternating, dialogic pieces. In the very last of these, a Complaint, the Lady proclaims her pain and foolishness.

A Courtly Romance

The Duke's story resembles many another courtly romance in that his love is expressed through a system of literary metaphors and arguments elaborated primarily in the twelfth and early thirteenth centuries, one that held a nostalgic, golden-age flavor for many readers in the fifteenth century. *The Book of the Duke of True Lovers* emphasizes some of courtly love's tenets. One of those is the concept of love as a malady authorizing the Duke to hope the Lady will save him from certain death (the "lady as doctor" theme); it includes the metaphor of love as a consuming flame, realized in the lover's alternating burning and thirst, and his paleness and high color.[5] Another entrenched courtly argument lies in the Duke's belief that the Lady's love will make him valorous, inspiring him to great deeds of chivalry, and that she will increase his worth by loving him. Such mainstays of the courtly edifice are eventually condemned in the *Duke of True Lovers,* in the Dame de la Tour's letter, which persuades the Lady for a very brief time to renounce her liaison. She writes to the Duke that Foolish Love caused in her a *nisse pitié,* "naïve pity," for his claims to be dying of love for her. And as for the argument that love makes a man worthier, the Dame de la Tour boldly declares that it hardly makes sense for a woman to ruin her reputation in order to enhance someone else's.

Conjoined with Christine's critique of adulterous love is a skepticism about the literature that glorifies it, which might be called upon to authorize it. Christine hints at that when the Duke says he desired to be a lover because he had heard "lovers praised more than other people." Perhaps what the Duke heard came from medieval courtly romance, among which the first part of *The Romance of the Rose* is an important example. The *Rose* is a two-part allegorical work created in two stages by two different, even conflicting, authors. The first (the "courtly" version) was composed in about 1225 by Guillaume de Lorris, the second (the larger "bourgeois" section) in about 1275 by Jean de Meun. The work remained influential through the fifteenth century. Christine's dislike of the work, especially Meun's part, had already been the grounds for her correspondence with a group of royal secretaries in an exchange now known as the "Debate of the Rose," (1401– 1404);[6] indeed, she even seems to allude to the dispute in one of the ballades in the *Duke of True Lovers:* "Freshly, newly/More than the rose,/Whose strife truly/I did disclose;/Piety chose;/A byegone case; Pray, grant me grace" (p. 96). Guillaume de Lorris's *Rose* tells the story of a young man who dreams he has gone out walking and come upon a garden where he falls in love with one single Rose, symbol of the beloved lady whose purity made her unattainable. Most scholars hold that Lorris died before finishing the *Rose*. In a very different spirit the irreverent Jean de Meun added more than 17,000 lines of learned discourse to Lorris's 4,000-line romance, bringing the work to its conclusion: in Jealousy's tower, where Rose has been imprisoned, the lover, "in no uncertain terms, deflowers the rose"[7]—a culmination Lorris does not seem to have envisaged.

Christine's arguments with Jean de Meun's work are by now well-known[8] and some of the dispute continues in *The Book of the Duke of True Lovers*. But Lorris's part of the work, a model of the courtly pursuit, is probably more germane. The garden of Lorris's *Rose,* its fountain, Cupid's arrow of Sweet Look and his Ten Commandments of Love, a code that includes advice on keeping well-dressed and well-groomed, have their echoes in the *Duke of True Lovers.* The retelling of the Narcissus myth in the *Rose,* the story of a young man who drowns trying to achieve the love he desires (that of his own reflection in the fountain), is also relevant to the *Duke of True Lovers* because the *Rose* narrator interprets it as a warning to ladies who would let their lovers die of yearning, and he apostrophizes them thus:[9]

> You ladies, who refuse to satisfy
> Your lovers, this one's case should take to heart;
> For, if you let your sweethearts die,
> God will know how to give you recompense. [10]

The characters of Jealousy and Danger (this latter often referring loosely to all the forces that endanger love) figure prominently in both the *Rose* and *The Book of the Duke of True Lovers.*

The Problem of Romance

Christine's awareness of the "politics of representation" at work in romance left her uncomfortable with a genre that was far from providing the sort of formative model she preferred. Yet, desiring to respect her noble patron and, no doubt, to honor certain expectations on the part of her readers, she generally depicts the Duke as well-meaning. He is not to be counted among "false lovers." When he spends money generously and cultivates excellent manners, hoping that people will speak well of him and that the Lady, hearing their words, will form a favorable impression, his efforts conform to the aristocratic, courtly prescription. Yet once the Dame de la Tour speaks out about the liaison, the Duke's preoccupations are subject to a re-reading. In that retrospective view, he appears self-absorbed: his desire to earn his manhood through his affair with the Lady marks him as, marginally, among the self-indulgent youth Christine had ridiculed elsewhere. [11]

In part, the Duke's youth is to blame. Like many of her contemporaries, Christine saw the follies of love as the province of the young. Carefree, restless, and blissfully unaware, the Duke sets out to hunt (for rabbits) but, in the terms of courtly romance's typical initial motif, Love overtakes him, and he becomes the hunter who is himself caught. (In addition to other twelfth- and thirteenth-century examples, Lorris's lover of *The Romance of the Rose* again springs to mind, a youth of twenty who also sets out one fine morning, only to be surprised by love.) The Duke cannot speak when he should, nor can he interpret the signs the lady gives. [12] His youth is enhanced further by a pair of uncommon details that emphasize his status as a young dependent of his parents: the Duke's worry that he will anger his father by returning home after dark; and, the pains he must take to obtain money for his expenses from his parents, especially his father, from whom he stands to inherit property.

The Duke's described initiation into manhood participates in an extensive literature of a young hero's education ranging from Virgil's epic poem *The Aeneid* to Chrétien de Troyes's *Perceval* in the twelfth century to Dante's *Divine Comedy* in the fourteenth (a favorite of Christine's). Accounts such as the Duke's also anticipate the *Bildungsroman* of later literature (that is, a novel about a young person's development out of the world of childhood). In a courtly romance like *The Book of the Duke of True Lovers,* the young man's initiation occurs through love and the Lady is its instrument; the romance is therefore not the story of the Lady's development. Indeed, in *The Book of the Duke of True Lovers,* the hero's education, his own ascent toward renown, and the Dame de la Tour's program for the Lady's honor, are entirely at cross-purposes.

But however neutrally the Duke's character may otherwise be presented, the stunning irruption into the poem of a letter from Sebille de Monthault, Dame de la Tour, leaves no doubt about how the story is to be read, at least where the Lady is concerned. Sebille had once been the Lady's governess, and now the Lady has asked her to return briefly to act as the sort of duenna the affair requires: someone whose presence would *seem* to assure the virtue of the young woman while in reality she is an accomplice to the Lady's adventures. Sebille refuses, saying that her ailing daughter requires her attention. With all due respect for the Lady's station, and in tones that recall Christine's own voice in *The Romance of the Rose* debate letters, the Dame de la Tour goes on to explain to the Lady how her conduct endangers her reputation. The letter thus ruptures the romance setting by placing the *speculum* of social reality against literary representation.

The Dame de la Tour's letter addresses the problem of romance on a few fronts. As a genre with a traditionally male perspective, the romance was deeply resistant to being rewritten from a woman's point of view. Christine's distaste for it, therefore, came not only from its dismaying ethics, but also from its exclusion of the possibility for innovation by women writers. [13] The story itself of the Lady's demise in the *Duke of True Lovers* rewrites the courtly romance after a fashion by emphasizing its harmful consequences for the Lady. But Christine must have felt the limitations of such a portrait, for it could provide no positive model, no example of what the Lady might instead strive for. Sebille's letter remedies that lack by interjecting an alternative program for the Lady.

The letter, a didactic treatise in prose, a literary vehicle that

Christine favored for moral reform especially after 1405, contrasts with and effectively breaks off the poetry of the romance, silencing it for a time. Its concern, different from that of the romance, lies in the moral education of *women,* on forming "women of honor." Casting Sebille de Monthault as the *Duke of True Lovers'* privileged writer/reader, therefore, Christine fills a role left open when she submerged her own voice in the Duke's. As the author's opinion of the Duke was left enigmatic, and the "meaning" of the tale left open, so the letter also serves as a gloss upon the hitherto-neutralized tale, in Christine's own language. Like the arrangement of text and gloss in Christine's otherwise quite different work, *The Epistle of Othea to Hector,* the idea, too, is not to leave the point of the story open to misreading. Since it is the Duke who reports on the letter's contents, Christine has arranged things so that a man is forced to read a woman reading a woman: woman glosses man.

Personal honor and renown were twin preoccupations all through the Middle Ages. Striving for praise (especially as depicted in the romance) was most often expected of men, who were to seek their reputations through chivalrous deeds among their fellow men, and the favor of their beloved. (In this the Duke is no exception.) With its emphasis upon honor for *women,* however, the Dame de la Tour's letter looks forward to Christine's even longer treatment of the subject in the *Book of the Three Virtues* (1405; also called *The Treasury of the City of Ladies*),[14] in which, in fact, the Dame de la Tour's letter is repeated. That work, probably written soon after the *Duke of True Lovers,* is a book of advice to women in three parts: the first addresses princesses and high-ranking ladies, the second, ladies and *damoiselles,* the third, city women, merchants' wives, and women of the common people. In the chapters devoted to the young, newly married noblewoman (Part One, Chapters 24–27),[15] Christine turns to advising the noble lady's duenna.

The importance of the lady's reputation is underlined by the somewhat unscrupulous means the duenna must adopt to prevent a liaison between the lady in her charge and any would-be lovers: after gaining the young man's confidence in order to learn his intentions, she will assure him that the lady has no interest whatsoever in him, and that if she did, she (the duenna) would intervene; the lady herself is not to know of the young man's suit, if possible, nor of the duenna's interventions. Should the duenna find herself advising an incorrigible lady, she will leave her service, saying that she must go by reason of poor health, or making some other excuse. Should she later hear that her young charge's honor has been impugned, she will write to her. At this point Sebille's letter is repeated, introduced in the following way: "it may happen that the young woman will behave so ill advisedly after the departure of the woman who used to be her governess that words will be uttered attacking her honor, and they will so multiply that the good and wise lady mentioned above, who had charge of her and now resides in her own household, will hear of it—at which she will be so unhappy to see her *mistress's honor* diminished, *she whom she had taken such pains to teach and educate well,* that she could not tolerate it" (italics mine).[16]

Sebille ends her letter in the *Duke of True Lovers* with the ballade "Women of Honor" *(Dames d'honneur),* a poem that Christine had written earlier and included in her collection of "Autres Balades."[17] Small but significant changes adapt the poem to the case of the Duke and Lady, making its lesson more immediate. When the Lady fails to heed Sebille's advice, her story becomes one of moral decline: she will not be a "woman of honor." Indeed, the defenseless and anxious Lady of the poem's end contrasts disturbingly with the balanced, intelligent, gracious woman who was once (in the garden scene) better able than the Duke to converse about foreign courts and governments.

The Old Woman

The Duke, not surprisingly, sees the Dame de la Tour as his

enemy, muttering about that "old woman." Yet he himself is tutored by a sort of male counterpart, a more experienced male cousin, who guides and educates him in the ways of love. At the same time the cousin's craftiness helps to preserve the Duke's own appearance of innocence, just as the duenna protects the Lady's own gentility. He perceives that the Duke is in love even before the Duke himself realizes. It is he, therefore, who tells the lovelorn and ailing Duke how to interpret his lady's behavior toward him. He arranges the lovers' first secret meeting, having spoken to the Lady on the Duke's behalf. He tells her that he has tried to dissuade the young man from his amorous pursuit (though, in truth of course, he had encouraged him). So it is the older man, more experienced in the ways of adultery than either the Duke or the Lady, who most resembles those feigning lovers Christine deplored. As Sebille's structural opposite, the Duke's cousin upholds the romance vision that she opposes.

The name Sebille de Monthault, Dame de la Tour, is a transparent reference to the wise sibyl, a figure of authority who appears in three of Christine's didactic works, *The Epistle of Othea to Hector* (1399–1400), the *Road of Long Learning* (1404), and in *The Book of the City of Ladies* (1404–05). [18] The idea of a sibyl's lofty wisdom, made public through pronouncements uttered from a high promontory, is doubly inscribed by *Mont hault,* "high mountain," and *de la Tour,* "of the tower." Like a sibyl, too, the "Lady of the Tower" is a visionary: she knows more than her ill-fated correspondent knows, and she correctly predicts the troubles that will ensue from the Lady's love affair with the Duke. Indeed, the love affair does not really begin to founder until the Dame de la Tour sends her letter.

Christine's deployment of wise women figures took more than one form. Boethius's *Consolation of Philosophy* (ca. 524) was an important influence on Sebille's characterization and on the prose of her intervention in an otherwise mostly poetic work (see translator's Note on the Lyric Poetry). [19] The old-young woman, the allegorical Lady Philosophy who appears to Boethius, in fact inspired a number of allegorical figures who advise Christine, authorized to do so by their divine origins.

Christine would have been nearly forty years old when she wrote the *Duke of True Lovers,* an older woman by medieval standards. She was well aware that medieval literature was generally unkind to the aged, especially aged women. In this a particularly influential offender was again *The Romance of the Rose,* in the form of Jean de Meun's allegorical Old Woman, or Duenna: a cynical, opportunistic creature who, when given the chance to advise a young woman about love, tells her to get what she can while she can, for youth and beauty soon fade. The flesh-and-blood realism of Meun's portraiture influenced Chaucer's shading of the Wife of Bath and Villon's "Regrets de la belle Healmière." The abiding popularity of Meun's view must have been a factor in Christine's desire to portray older women of wisdom and value, antidotes to Meun's depiction.

Tales of Love

Christine's writing career at the time of the *Duke of True Lover's* composition certainly supports her claim that courtly romance held less interest for her than other subjects. Between ca. 1394 and 1400, when she was beginning her career as a writer and hoped to attract patrons, love had been her most important (though not exclusive) subject. She treated it in her first collection of lyric poems, the *Hundred Ballades,* and in her *Virelais, Rondeaux, Autres Ballades,* and in three narrative poems on love questions composed c. 1400: *The Debate of Two Lovers, The Book of Three Judgments,* and *The Tale of Poissy.*[20] But beginning in 1399 with *The Letter of the God of Love,* and followed in 1401–04 by the Debate letters, Christine began to turn to more serious themes. By 1405 she had written a number of learned works, some quite lengthy: the *Epistle of Othéa to Hector* (1399–1400); *Moral Teachings* and *Moral Proverbs* (1400–01); *The Book of the Road of Long Learning*

(1402–03); *The Book of the Mutation of Fortune* (1403); *The Book of Human Integrity* (1403–04); *The Book of the Deeds and Good Customs of the Wise King Charles V* (1404); *The Book of the City of Ladies* (1404–05); *The Book of the Three Virtues,* or *The Treasury of the City of Ladies* (1405); and, the *Avision-Christine* (1405).²¹ Only three times in the years following 1400, in fact, did Christine depart from that scholarly program to write "tales of love": *The Tale of the Shepherdess* (1403), *The Book of the Duke of True Lovers* (1403–05) and *The Hundred Ballades of Lover and Lady* (1409–10). She did not return to the subject at any length after 1410.

Almost all of Christine's narrative poems on cases of love raise questions but avoid answering them—a general rule to which *The Book of the Duke of True Lovers,* because of the Dame de la Tour's letter, constitutes an exception. The "judgment" poems written c. 1400 *(The Book of the Three Judgments, The Tale of Poissy,* and *The Debate of Two Lovers)* are so called because in them an eminent person is asked to decide who is right in various matters of love, although the judgments are never recorded. *The Tale of the Shepherdess* (1403), in which Christine depicts the sad consequences for a young peasant woman of her affair with a knight, may be regarded as Christine's anti-*pastourelle.*²² Of all these *The Debate of Two Lovers* in particular offers an enlightening perspective on *The Book of the Duke of True Lovers.*

The occasion for the debate is a ball where Christine observes two young knights: one, like Christine herself, remains uninvolved in the festivities, and he looks quite sad; the other is dancing and enjoying himself. Eventually the two knights, along with Christine, decide to debate their opposing views of love. Before they withdraw to an orchard to do so, Christine invites two more women, identified only as a *dame* of unspecified age, and a *bourgeoise,* a merchant's wife or citywoman, to join them. Once in the orchard, the unhappy knight avers that Jealousy is inevitable in love, and he advances the classically male view that the jealous lover is "more of a slave than a dog on a leash held by the hunter" (ll. 625–26). To support his views he cites the cases of famous lovers from classical and medieval literature who were ruined by love.[23]

Before the second knight responds, the lady who had been invited along comments on the first knight's argument. Her appearance there, speaking as an invited outsider, and the points she makes, though delivered in little more than eighty lines (ll. 921–1000), constitute a sketchy precursor of Sebille de Monthault as "invited outsider." She declares that there are really very few lovers who are prisoners of love, but "that's a very common *conte*, a tale told to women," and, "she who believes it in the end is not considered very wise" (ll. 936–37; 939–41). Talking of love like that is just a current fad *(usage)*, done for amusement and to pass the time (ll. 942–44). It may once have been true that lovers were so loyal, but that has not been the case for more than a hundred years (ll. 945–50). Now lovers depend on glib talk (ll. 950–951) and their pain is quite small—though it is described at length in romances *(romans)* (ll. 957–958). There are few lovers like the one in *The Romance of the Rose,* for nowadays they want only easy living. Besides, she asks, who can live in the sort of discomfort that the first knight has described? What man can bear it? And then, where, in the cemetery, are the graves of those who actually died of loving?

In the longest speech of the work, the second knight argues that love makes a man valorous—look at Lancelot (1425–1438), or a number of real-life exemplars. In the end Christine suggests that they submit the case to the Duke of Orleans. Nevertheless, in the speech of the unidentified *dame* the author has had *her* say.

Once more after writing the *Duke of True Lovers* Christine took up the matter of courtly love. Her *Hundred Ballades of Lover and Lady* of 1409–10,[24] which she claims once more to have written to satisfy the request of a noble person, is a lovers' dialogue in which the story unfolds in the alternating ballades of Lover and Lady.[25] The work represents a culmination of Christine's treatment in dialogue of the love theme. She had begun writing lovers' dialogues in short poems as early as her first collection of lyric poems, the *Hundred Ballades,* and her predilection for narrating dialogically appears throughout her poetic writing. It reappears in the *Duke of True Lovers* in the exchange of letters between Lover and Lady, in the poem's unusual casting of their first secret conversation as a dialogue that consecrates the moment, in the Duke's poetry throughout the story, but especially in the Lovers' lyrics of the poem's poetic coda—this last already moving toward the sophisticated, entirely balladic, narrative of *The Hundred Ballades of Lover and Lady.*[26]

In that work the Lady disdains the Lover for a time, but eventually she too yields to the urgency of his entreaties. The one-hundredth and final ballade is uttered by the Lady, too enfeebled by her chagrin to leave her bed. Here Christine again turns the tables, showing that Love's malady, conceived of as afflicting men, affects women too. Thus *The Hundred Ballades of Lover and Lady,* which Christine claimed to have written to make amends for *The Book of the Duke of True Lovers,*[27] in fact returns to the same conclusion offered in the earlier work.

The Theme of the Refusal of Love

The refusal of adulterous passion that Christine advocated enjoyed a rich posterity. In 1424,[28] at a time when Christine herself had ceased writing, Alain Chartier composed his *Belle Dame sans mercy,* oddly destined to become better-known than Christine's writings on the subject, yet echoing them closely. Chartier must have met Christine in Paris between 1410 and 1418, and Christine's son, Jean du Castel, was a colleague of Chartier's in the chancellery. The Belle Dame, unlike any of Christine's heroines, succeeds in refusing love; her suitor, though an exemplary courtly supplicant, fails to move her. She thinks instead about false lovers who betray their ladies and boast of their conquests, the kind whom Christine herself had condemned. When the lover claims that his pain is caused by the lady's beauty and cruelty, the Belle Dame retorts that, on the contrary, his suffering is his own fault. Even when the lover appeals to Death to deliver him, the lady remains inflexible, finally growing short-tempered and brusque. When Chartier's lover begs the lady to remember Pity, she replies that "Pity must be reasonable/And harmful to none . . . If a lady is pitying toward others/Only to be cruel to herself,/Her pity is to be despised"[29]—precisely the point that Sebille had already made.

Why, then, are there so few examples in Christine's poetry of heroines who succeed[30] in refusing love? Part of the answer can be found in a comparison of her heroine with Chartier's: despite their apparent similarities, Chartier's heroine is rather in the tradition of the inaccessible courtly lady, essentially a masculine conception of woman. Christine had a very different idea about what she called the *nature de femme.* She wrote:

> For woman's nature is but sweet and mild,
> Compassionate and fearful, timorous
> And humble, gentle, sweet, and generous,
> And pleasant, pious, meek in time of peace,
> Afraid of war, religious, plain at heart.
> When angry, quickly she allays her ire,
> Nor can she bear to see brutality
> Or suffering. It's clear those qualities
> By nature make a woman's character.
> And she who's lacking them by accident
> Corrupts her nature, goes against the grain.
> In women cruelty's to be reproved,
> And gentleness alone should be approved. (ll. 668–80)[31]

Christine was a humanist who shared with her contemporaries a belief in human nature and a desire to speculate about it. She was consistent in depicting that type of innocent (and generally young), compliant woman, who is present from her earliest narrative poetry, beginning with the "simple virgin," Rose, of the *Romance of the Rose* (whom Cupid defends in *The Letter of the God of Love*) and ending in 1429 when life startlingly provided a real, young and honorable heroine, Joan of Arc, whose cause Christine came out of her tacit retirement to champion in the *Poem of Joan of Arc*. Thus, though the haughty *domna* of courtly poetry was able to resist Love's seductions and imperious command, Christine's idea of a young woman was of someone too artless, too fundamentally kind—too averse to cruelty—to say no.

Here again, therefore, in a characteristic move, Christine reverses the terms of the argument: though male authors thought that men suffered in love as victims of the only conception of woman that the courtly model allowed (the inaccessible one), Christine argued that it was in fact the woman who would suffer in illicit relationships.

A much later French work in this tradition is of course Madame de Lafayette's *Princess of Clèves*, written in 1678. Situated at the court of Henri II (1547–59), this early psychological novel was actually written during the reign of Louis XIV and refers to the latter's court. In a narrative often ruled largely by direct discourse, Madame de Lafayette embeds hearsay within hearsay, anecdote within anecdote, to recreate life at Versailles in the seventeenth century—a court not entirely without its parallels in the fifteenth century. Rivalry and intrigue, and with them dissimulation, are the central business of the court's occupants, along with attendance at official ceremonies. Like *The Book of the Duke of True Lovers*, the *Princess of Clèves* takes as one of its themes the moral education of a young woman, for it is due to the principles inculcated by her mother, Mme. de Chartres, that the Princess rejects the values of the court, and with them the handsome Duke of Nemours. Though the Princess and Duke are powerfully drawn to one another, their love remains unfulfilled. The relationship in the *Princess of Clèves* between Mme. de Chartres and her daughter cannot help but recall that of the Dame de la Tour and the Lady in *The Book of the Duke of True Lovers* (in fact, the Lady refers to the Dame de la Tour both as her mother and adoptive mother). It is worth noting that although the Princess of Clèves refuses love, the novel repeatedly emphasizes how unique and atypical that refusal (and her unprecedented confession to her husband, which causes his death) makes her,[32] a solitary person withdrawn from her society. The depiction suggests the general difficulty of refusal from a woman writer's perspective, and that it was perhaps not as easily done as Chartier would have it.

Social Tableau

The Book of the Duke of True Lovers is a lively representation of late medieval aristocratic life. The pageantry of tournament and feast was much favored by Christine's patrons, the ruling House of Orleans and its rivals, the Burgundians, who were renowned for the magnificence of their celebrations. The King himself, Charles VI, had been a great lover of tournaments at the beginning of his reign. In 1389, for example, he participated in the three-day jousts at St. Denis, held after his wife Isabeau was crowned queen of France. Their contemporary, the chronicler Froissart, reports that the ladies, who were watching from the scaffolds erected above the lists, judged the winner (with the heralds), just as they do in the *Duke of True Lovers*.[33]

A revelry like the one the Duke undertakes would have been too costly, even for the very rich, to be an everyday event. The Duke spends vast sums of money to outfit his own team of twenty in silk of gold and green (the color of love and of spring), and his provision to them of costumes all in the same colors shows that they are "brothers in arms for the occasion."[34]

The setting for the tournament is not less attractive. In the field where the jousts take place—a *locus amoenus* with a view of a six-turreted castle and a pond—there are pavilions, large tents made of expensive fabric whose center pole could have flown the Duke's banner. When the company approach the field they see chargers with high saddles painted red, white, and green, and decorated with emblems. The lances are also painted, and are thus of the most expensive kind.

Certain details of tournament procedure may be glimpsed in Christine's account. Unseating an opponent, for example, earned the highest marks, while the breaking of many lances was prized (especially the more ornate ones), as was the striking of the visor. Heralds, under marshals, regulated tournaments, and trumpets announced the entrance of each new contestant.

Such tableaus once more show Christine's expertise at visual evocation, a talent that had emerged earlier in, for instance, the *Tale of the Rose* (1402), where a dazzling dinner party is followed by an equally brilliant dream vision; or, in *The Tale of Poissy,* which contains a fascinating description of the abbey's architecture and the lives of its inhabitants. Combined with the use of spoken genres (such as lyric poetry, dialogues, and the like), this sort of narrated performance points to Christine's predilection for the drama of staged fictions.

Several references to Germany and German customs would have reminded medieval readers that Queen Isabeau, wife of Charles VI, came from Bavaria, a member of the powerful Wittelsbach family. The revelers at the Duke's ball prepare to dance the *Allemande;* the winner of the prize for those not from the region is a German; the Duke's cousin travels between France and Germany; and ballade IX in the sequence of poems at the end has the Duke himself about to return to France from Germany—about to leave the "Teutonic tongue" and the land of beer, as he puts it.

Although these references appear in both manuscripts containing the poem, the later of the two was commissioned by the Queen (see manuscripts discussion, below). The name of Isabeau of Bavaria has not fared well in accounts of French history, for a number of reasons. One of those is her alleged infidelity to the king, perhaps encouraged by Charles VI's bouts of insanity, the first of which occurred in 1392. The advice given especially to "high-ranking princesses," whose every gesture is noted by all around them, as Sebille writes, may well have had some relevance to Isabeau's situation.

The Book of the Duke of True Lovers is found in the Bibliothèque Nationale's MS f.fr. 836 (ca. 1407–08) and the British Library's Harley MS 4431 (ca. 1410–15). Christine issued her first collection of works in 1402, before the poem was written, and thus it does not appear in her earlier manuscripts.

MS 836, part of a group with MSS B.N. f.fr. 835, 605, and 606, was prepared for Louis, Duke of Orleans, brother of King Charles VI. It was purchased after Louis's death (1407) by Jean, Duke of Berry.

Of the two luxurious manuscripts, the Harley, commissioned by Queen Isabeau, is the more substantial collection. It was prepared under Christine's supervision, and she may well have copied portions of it herself.[35] It is graced by numerous skillful illustrations, striking for their vivid color, careful line, and freshly-painted quality. Six accompany the text of the *Duke of True Lovers*, an unusually high number when we consider that each of the other courtly narrative poems in the collection has but one illustration, and a much longer work, *The Book of the City of Ladies*, contains only three.

The illustrations tell the story of love's progress, constituting in themselves a nearly independent visual performance that enhances the narrated one.[36] The first shows the Duke making his request of Christine (Fig. 1), while the remaining five depict scenes typical to the romance: the hunt (Fig. 2), the conversation in the garden (Fig. 3), the tournament (Fig. 4), the Lady taking leave of the Duke's residence (Fig. 5), and the Duke lamenting to his cousin (Fig. 6); exceptionally, this last has a caption. Not remarkably, perhaps, the Dame de la Tour's portrait is omitted.

Although the Harley 4431 and its miniature paintings have been the subject of scholarly studies, none, to my knowledge, has concentrated on its distinctive depictions of clothing and costume. These are especially noteworthy in light of the fact that though the Hundred Years' War (1337–1453) had prevented

France from fully developing its textile industry, a spurt of interest in luxurious apparel, probably encouraged by Queen Isabeau's lavish tastes, occurred in France at the time of the Harley manuscript's preparation.[37]

In the six Harley illustrations for *The Book of the Duke of True Lovers* men outnumber women significantly, and their costumes, especially those of the Duke, are more elaborate and varied. In the first illustration the Duke wears a houppelande, a copious outer garment said to have been fashionable during the reign of Charles VI.[38] It featured generally wide sleeves and a high, fitted collar. The Duke's houppelande is of a deep orange color and is trimmed in gold (Fig. 1); great expense is exhibited in its excessively long and wide sleeves, dagged and turned back to reveal their generous fur lining. His hose is parti-colored (that is, each leg is a different, contrasting color). In all, the sumptuousness of his ensemble in this initial portrayal contrasts with the simplicity of Christine's own garments.

The Duke's elegant tenue of course suits his station. Although his head is bare in the first illustration, in the hunting scene (Fig. 2) he sports a twisted and snipped capuchon, one of three intriguing headdresses he is portrayed wearing.[39] His houppelande is suitably short for riding but still fur-lined, and its sleeves and hems are dagged. In the garden scene (Fig. 3), he is wearing an elaborate hat made of peacock feathers.[40] When the Duke is seen languishing in bed, however, confiding his anguish to his cousin (Fig. 6), he wears a blue houppelande and a hood arranged as a hat. An anlace, or dagger, hangs at his side.

As for the Lady, she appears in three illustrations: in the gallery at the tournament scene (Fig. 4), in the garden (Fig. 3), and in a scene depicting her departure from the Duke's castle (Fig. 5). Except in the tournament scene, where she is attired in white and gold, she wears a blue houppelande (blue was the color of loyalty, as nos. 91 and 92 of *The Hundred Ballades of Lover and Lady* testify[41]; Christine herself is most often depicted wearing blue). On the Lady's head is a *bourrelet,* a rolled headdress.

The Paris manuscript contains illustrations of the same scenes as those in the Harley. Nevertheless, the costumes, and especially those of the Duke, are less extravagant.

The Harley illustrator's work is also noteworthy for its faithfulness to the text itself. Two instances should be mentioned. First, the text says that at the tournament the ladies are wearing white and gold, and indeed, the Harley illustrations show them in ensembles of white and gold. A knight sports a green and gold outfit, and two of the ladies wear headdresses of green and gold, thus carrying through the Duke's color scheme. On the ground lies one broken lance—a red one and thus one belonging to an opponent (since the Duke's are white). In the Paris manuscript, on the other hand, the ladies are dressed in red or blue. Second, when the Duke relates his sad tale to his cousin, he instructs him to "lean a bit closer." In the Harley manuscript illustration, the cousin leans to his left, toward the Duke, with his elbow on the arm of the chair. In the Paris manuscript, however, the cousin is pictured sitting upright.

About the Translation

The present translation has been made from the text of the poem contained in the Harley manuscript 4431.

Although the octosyllable was traditional in the romance, the more than 3550 lines of *The Book of the Duke of True Lovers* are heptasyllables, a meter that Christine used in a number of instances. Lines rhyme in couplets, in the rich "leonine" rhyme Christine refers to at the end of the poem. The correspondence is in prose. (See "A Note on the Translation of the Lyric Poetry," which follows.)

This translation into prose of both the narrative poetic portion of the text and the prose letters aims at a contemporary English free of archaisms. The long sentences and embedded clauses of the French text, which occur in the metrical narrative but more markedly in the prose letters, have been simplified in English, and the French text's very frequent use of connectives such as "and" and "so" to introduce new sentences has been adapted to more modern English usage. Verb tenses have been made to agree with one another more often than they do in the French poem.

The black-and-white reproductions of the Harley illustrations to *The Book of the Duke of True Lovers* are placed here approximately where they occur in the manuscript text itself.

An earlier English translation of the *Duke of True Lovers* was published in 1908 by Alice Kemp-Welch (reprint 1966), with lyric poetry translated by Laurence Binyon and Eric R. D. Maclagan. It is rendered in a deliberately archaic English and, without explanation, does not include the sequence of poems following the end of the Duke's story.

In this translation the numbers in parentheses at the conclusion of most paragraphs refer to line numbers in a new edition of the *Livre du Duc des vrais amans* that I am now preparing. These correspond to line numbers in Maurice Roy's edition (*Oeuvres poétiques de Christine de Pisan,* Vol. 3, 59–208) with the following alterations: in the new edition the two rondeaus each have one extra line, thus adding one, then two, to the continuous numbering; further, I have allowed a line number for the missing line at (my no.) 2069, so that after that point my edition has three more lines than Roy's.

—Thelma Fenster
Fordham University, 1991

NOTES

1. In these notes shortened bibliographic citations are used; complete information for all items may be found in the Selective Bibliography. I thank Roberta Krueger and Nadia Margolis for reading and commenting most helpfully upon an earlier draft of this introduction.

    For details of Christine's life (1365–1430?) the reader is invited to consult Charity Cannon Willard, *Christine de Pizan, Her Life and Works.*

2. Liliane Dulac, "Christine de Pisan et le malheur des *vrais amans,*" p. 227.

3. Dulac argues that the dilemma into which the Duke's request plunged Christine—

how to "reconcile two contradictory moral philosophies"—is handled by creating a difference between the fates of Duke and Lady. In a subtle discussion, Dulac finds that Christine's attitude toward the Duke is complex and less clear than her view of the Lady: the Duke's "malady" is cured only at the Lady's expense, for the generosity that was the cause of her greatness is at the same time her undoing.

4. The Duke says that during the first two years of the affair, the Lady would not let him leave the country (l. 3354). He says he was then in Spain for one year (l. 3431), and that his life of "coming and going" (which may or may not include the trip to Spain) lasted for ten years (l. 3455).

5. Such images may of course be found among the classical Latin writers, particularly Ovid, whose depictions of love were absorbed into the medieval courtly repertory.

6. See *Le Débat sur le Roman de la Rose,* Eric Hicks, ed., which is the definitive edition of all the Debate documents; or *La Querelle de la Rose: Letters and Documents,* Joseph L. Baird and John R. Kane, eds., which has English translations of the Debate documents based on an earlier edition now superseded by Hicks's edition.

7. David F. Hult, "Jean de Meun's Continuation of *Le roman de la rose,*" p. 99.

8. See my synopsis of the arguments in the introduction to *Poems of Cupid, God of Love: Christine de Pizan's "Epistre au dieu d'Amours" and "Dit de la Rose"; Thomas Hoccleve's "The Letter of Cupid"; with George Sewell's "The Proclamation of Cupid,"* p. 6.

9. See Daniel Poirion's "Narcisse et Pygmalion dans le *Roman de la Rose,*" and his discussion of the work in *Le Roman de la Rose.*

10. *The Romance of the Rose,* tr. Harry Robbins, p. 31.

11. In the *Letter of the God of Love,* for example; *Poems of Cupid,* pp. 35–37.

12. Nadia Margolis has commented informally that in this respect the Duke is like Perceval in the Grail story: too literal-minded to interpret words and signs, Perceval commits a series of blunders, including failing to ask the one question that would release the Fisher King from his bondage.

13. Nadia Margolis calls attention to the intractability of romance and the greater malleability of medieval historiography, a genre that therefore appealed much more to Christine ("Christine de Pizan: The Poetess as Historian," p. 365). Roberta Krueger discusses Christine's rewriting of romance in *The Book of the Duke of True Lovers* through the character of the Lady but especially through the Dame de la Tour's letter; Krueger suggests, however, that the program the Dame de la Tour advocates is constricting in its own way ("A Woman's Response: Christine de Pizan's *Le Livre du Duc des vrais amants* and the Limits of Romance," in *The Lady in the Frame: Women Readers and Twelfth- and Thirteenth-Century Old French Verse Romance* [provisional title]; forthcoming.)

14. There are two English translations: *Christine de Pisan, The Treasure of the City of Ladies,* tr. Sarah Lawson; and, *A Medieval Woman's Mirror of Honor: The Treasury of the City of Ladies,* tr. Charity Cannon Willard, ed. Madeleine Pelner Cosman.

15. *Christine de Pizan, Le Livre des Trois Vertus. Edition critique.* Ed. Charity Cannon Willard, with Eric Hicks, pp. 90–120; *A Medieval Woman's Mirror of Honor,* pp. 125–147.

16. My translation from *Christine de Pizan, Le Livre des Trois Vertus,* pp. 109–110.

17. Dulac points out that the poem as it appears in *The Book of the Duke of True Lovers*

is more serious, and the advice it gives is more urgent and categorical (p. 231).

18. It was the Cumaean Sibyl in particular who attracted Christine's attention. In Nadia Margolis's view Christine "took on the qualities of the Cumaean Sibyl, who led Aeneas to the underworld and who, in another thread of tradition, offered prophetic books to Tarquin the Proud." In Christine's writing "sibyls and sibylline figures" foretell the "Golden Age of Rome as coming to France rather than remaining in Italy," and in the *Epistre d'Othea* the Sibyl predicts "not only this triumph of *translatio studii* (with an eye toward *translatio imperii*) but also the growing role of women in shaping the New Order." ("Christine de Pizan: The Poetess as Historian," p. 363). (It was the Cumaean Sibyl who, as recorded in the *Epistre d'Othea,* announced the coming of Christ to the emperor Augustus.) Several scholars, following upon George Bumgardner's discussion in "Tradition and Modernity from 1380 to 1405: Christine de Pizan," pp. 105–131, and Nadia Margolis, "The Poetics of History: An Analysis of Christine de Pizan's *Livre de la Mutacion de Fortune,*" esp. pp. 8–9, think that Christine saw her own transplantation from Italy to France when still a very young child as an incarnation of the medieval idea of *translatio studii,* the carrying forth of culture from the ancient world to the modern.

19. See Howard Patch, *The Tradition of Boethius; A Study of His Importance in Medieval Culture,* and Glynnis Cropp, "Boèce et Christine de Pizan."

20. In *Oeuvres poétiques de Christine de Pisan,* ed. Maurice Roy, vol. 2: *Le Debat de deux amans,* pp. 49–109; *Le Livre des trois jugemens,* pp. 111–157; *Le Livre du dit de Poissy,* pp. 159–222. *Le Dit de la Pastoure* is also in vol. 2, pp. 223–294. There are as yet no English translations of these poems.

21. Only the *Epistle of Othea to Hector, The Book of the City of Ladies,* and *The Book of the Three Virtues* have been translated into English.

22. The pastourelle is a medieval genre in which a knight errant woos a shepherdess, usually seducing and then abandoning her. Christine's emphasis is of course upon the grieving of the shepherdess: Marote has given herself to the knight against the advice of her best friend, Lorete, who warns that Marote can never hope for a lasting relationship with the knight because of the difference in their social classes.

23. Some of the medieval romances he mentions (ll. 746–774) might well be the ones that offer "much praise" of lovers, for they have in common their sympathy for adulterous, courtly lovers. They include the famous Tristan and Yseut story and two thirteenth-century courtly romances, the *Chatelain de Couci* and the *Chatelaine de Vergi.* Roberta Krueger argues that these last two romances may in fact have served as models that Christine resisted and recast in *The Book of the Duke of True Lovers* (see n. 13).

24. *Cent Ballades d'amant et de dame,* Jacqueline Cerquiglini, ed., supersedes Maurice Roy's edition in his *Oeuvres poétiques de Christine de Pisan,* Vol. 3. There is no English translation.

25. See Charity Cannon Willard, "Christine de Pizan's *Cent Ballades d'amant et de dame:* Criticism of Courtly Love," and "Lovers' Dialogues in Christine de Pizan's Lyric Poetry from the *Cent Ballades* to the *Cent Ballades d'amant et de dame.*"

26. Suzanne Bagoly, "Christine de Pizan et l'art de 'dictier' ballades," p. 48.

27. *Cent Ballades d'amant et de dame,* p. 32.

28. For points made in this discussion of Chartier see the introduction to *Poèmes d'Alain Chartier*, James Laidlaw, ed., esp. pp. 13–14, 24–25.

29. *Poèmes d'Alain Chartier*, p. 180 (my translation).

30. There are some who refuse—for instance, a lady given voice in nos. 48 and 49 of the *Hundred Ballades*, Christine's earliest work.

31. *Letter of the God of Love*, in *Poems of Cupid*, p. 67.

32. A brief introduction to this work is given by John D. Lyons in *A New History of French Literature*, pp. 350–354.

33. Jean Froissart, *Oeuvres*, ed. Kervyn de Lettenhove, XIV 20–25, as cited in Richard Barber and Juliet Barker, *Tournaments: Jousts, Chivalry and Pageants in the Middle Ages*, p. 43.

34. Juliet R.V. Barker, *The Tournament in England 1100–1400*, p. 100. The custom of bestowing rich fabric or ensembles is well-documented: in May 1399, for example, the king issued green May Day livery to the men of the royal family and 200 others. In 1401 the queen gave all the ladies of her household a livery of blue cloth on the birth of her child (Joan Evans, *Dress in Mediaeval France*, pp. 39–40).

35. Gilbert Ouy and Christine Reno, "Identification des Autographes de Christine de Pizan" is a pioneering article about Christine's actual handwriting. Charity Cannon Willard was the first to suggest that another manuscript, Bibliothèque Nationale f. fr. 580, is an autograph manuscript ("An Autograph Manuscript of Christine de Pizan?" *Studi Francesi*, 27 [1965], 452–457).

36. For a discussion of writing and performance in the later Middle Ages, see Sylvia Huot, *From Song to Book. The Poetics of Writing in Old French Lyric and Lyrical Narrative Poetry*.

37. A second renewal of interest in elegant dressing occurred at the end of the war, in the 1450s (Doreen Yarwood, *European Costume. 4000 Years of Fashion*, p. 66).

38. Evans, p. 49.

39. This picture is sketched and described in Mary G. Houston, *Medieval Costume in England and France, the 13th, 14th and 15th Centuries*, p. 169.

40. The Duke's hat is significant enough to have been mentioned by Evans, p. 51.

41. *Cent Ballades d'amant et de dame*, pp. 122–123.

A Note on the Translation of the Lyric Poetry

The lyric poems (ballades, rondeaux, virelais, and complainte), have been translated while retaining their original *forme fixe* rhyme and metrical schemes. We have decided to differentiate between the two main poetic modes, lyric and narrative, via verse and prose rendering, respectively—in addition to the prose letters—to allow English readers to appreciate to a fuller extent the rich textuality of the *Duke of True Lovers*. It should be noted in this regard that Christine used Boethius's *Consolation of Philosophy* for its mixture of styles as well as for its philosophical theme, as she combined the elements of *prosimetrum* (prose and verse) with elements from the more conventional courtly romance, moral treatise, and epistolary novel—a late-medieval *Liaisons Dangereuses*.

Upon closer reading, the forms of poetic discourse in this work are more diverse than the simple narrative/lyric dualism noted at the outset. The lyric component comprises nineteen ballades, rondeaux, and virelais interspersed throughout the main body of the text, and thereafter the prologue, the sequence of nine ballades, three virelais, and four rondeaux, ending with the "complainte." These are all known as the *formes fixes*, especially the first three, and by Christine's time, the rules for composition had been well codified, and they continued to be used even through the modern period.

A preliminary, simplified review of terminology might help the reader more easily appreciate Christine's innovations in these forms while at the same time demonstrating the extent to which she worked within a prescribed tradition. As the hallmark genres of late medieval lyric, the fixed forms derive from *chansons à refrain* (songs with refrains); the ballade being the most flexible and most suitable for complex themes; the virelai most resembling a kind of dance (indeed, also called a *balette,* or *ballade balladant,* "ballad on a stroll") in its interlacing refrain, while the rondeau is the simplest, shortest, most self-contained—with potential for keen intensity. A representative sample scheme for each genre is provided below, although Christine and her contemporaries deviated from these at times:

> **Ballade:** 3 stanzas of 6-12 or more lines (7-10 syllables each), each ending with a refrain. At the end of the ballade traditionally is an envoi: homage to the poet's patron or to the subject of the poem. Typical rhyme schemes for each stanza (capital letter = refrain): ababbcaC, or ababccdD.
>
> **Rondeau** (often, in English, "Roundel"): 8-14 or more lines, first lines or part of them become refrain and coda, pursuing such rhyme schemes as: ABB ab AB abb ABB, or ABba abA abbaAB.
>
> **Virelai:** 1-3 stanzas (Christine preferred 2), each enclosed within the refrain, i.e., refrain-stanza-refrain-stanza-refrain, each grouping according to such rhyme schemes as ABBA cd, or AABBA bba. In the fifteenth century, the virelai came to resemble the rondeau.
>
> **Complainte:** Another courtly genre flourishing in the fifteenth century, this was not limited to the subject of love (the more "feminine" type, as in Machaut's *Voir Dit* ["True Tale"] of 1364); it also was used in political lament, to decry existing socio-historical conditions and pray for reform (the more "masculine" complaint). Rhyme scheme example: aaabaaabbbbabbba cccdcccddddcdddc, etc., with no refrain. Lines of alternating groups in length varying between 4-8 syllables.

Within the literary-historical perspective, again highly simplified, Christine belongs to a great tradition, that of the *grand chant courtois* ("grand courtly lyric"), whose exponents sought to cultivate and reconcile the themes of surprise (by Cupid upon the lover), joy, suffering, and death as essential themes in representing the meaning and ontology of love. To engage the courtly audience more easily, the poets would coin certain terms for these and related ideas and consistently repeat them as code words, to be rewoven into the continually renewed contexts and story-lines of the love affair being recreated in each poem. Contests were even held for such poets at the royal courts to foster refinement and variety within these highly ritualized genres. Adam de la Halle (1235–ca. 1285) is usually credited with first writing in the ballade form now known, although the influential composer and poet Guillaume de Machaut (ca. 1300–1377) established all of them in both literary theory and practice. Machaut served as a primary poetic mentor for Christine and her contemporaries: Deschamps, Froissart; then later, Charles d'Orléans and François Villon.

By Christine's time, *cri de cour* and *cri de coeur* had combined forces particularly in the very supple complainte and also in the ballade, allowing for extended thematic development and a highly individualized personal voice for the poet. Christine perhaps could be said to have exercised this freedom much more ardently than her contemporaries, even in the most rigid fixed forms or in her earlier, much longer *Mutation of Fortune* (1403) and others, as she often sought to merge historical events with the inner tumult of her narrator. Her lyric poems of historical-polemical interest usually stress the emotional side of her subject, while the book-length verse narrations, though not devoid of sentiment, emphasize her attempts at finding a rational system of causality and positive outlook for the future of France as well as her own. We would thus expect her to exploit the complainte at the end of *True Lovers* to the fullest.

At first reading, however, this complainte astounds us by its apparent self-confinement to the woman's unfortunate love affair. Yet it is nonetheless powerful, since the woman's bitter despondency convincingly suffices as its own universe. This centralized courtly theme, which ceremoniously thrusts the most sacred private emotion under public scrutiny and potential persecution, is revitalized by Christine as her narrator deplores, rather than celebrates, the ethos of courtliness for what she sees as its inherent hypocrisy. In the final analysis, then, Christine indeed follows the polemical (stereotypically masculine) tradition of complaint by presenting the affair as an example of the politics of love and not merely as an isolated tale of personal suffering.

Some of the fixed-form lyrics in the *Duke of True Lovers* may have been set pieces composed before Christine had the opportunity or sense of purpose to conceive the larger work, as hinted at in the rather convoluted opening lines of the narrative. Others appear distinctly to function as not much more than emphatic fillers or verbal filigrees to heighten a moment or facet in the emotional development of the story-line, just as one finds in modern operas and musicals. While several of the former type can stand alone as outstanding examples of Christine's contribution to late medieval verse, the latter category, quite adequate in their context, are simply not great poetry. In general, and regardless of quality, the lyric poems of the *Duke of True Lovers* should be judged more as a sort of courtly patter: thematically banal, they nevertheless captivate by their often monosyllabic incantation of love casuistry. As part of the narrative progression such poems act more as a mimesis of a love affair, with all of its conflicts, complexities, and vagaries—rather than elucidating or culminating in great philosophical ideas such as one would find in Petrarch or Dante. As examples of *formes fixes,* even the least successful represent Christine's uneasy relationship with the existing poetic genres of her time, as evidenced in her simultaneous mockery and manipulation of their constraints upon her as artistic innovator, particularly one in search of a woman's lyric discourse.

The above-mentioned stylistic, thematic, and literary-historical factors all generate concerns and challenges for the translator. They serve as enlightening additions to the more customary problem of preserving lexical and metrical fidelity to the original French text, in the endeavor, as an overall goal of the translation, to reproduce the freshness and grace of Christine's poetic voice as well as her message.

Especially in the shorter verses, this has not been a simple task, for the need to use subject pronouns in English where the Middle French requires none accounts for difficulties in simultaneously maintaining clarity and prescribed syllable length. This and similar grammatical obstacles occur even before those encountered in finding proper equivalents for the repetitious courtly code words, which often have polyvalent meanings.

In seeking to reproduce the balance between poetic message and stylistic virtuosity, should one of these be sacrificed to some degree, the translator must decide whether a poem is more important for its content or for its style, as in the two main categories discussed above, and render it accordingly. Thus, if some of the English rhymes seem overly playful or even forced, it is because I felt that this best communicated the essentially ludic quality of that poem, for Christine was capable of poetic gameplay through tears. By the same token, when obliged to opt for conveying the poem's message, I have sacrificed word-for-word faithfulness in favor of analogous expressions or entire ideas within a verse or more. In some poems, the apparent flaws are characteristic of the original: excessive monosyllables, twisted syntax, abuse of enjambement. The present translation does not undertake to smooth these over for the sake of finesse, since the poetic voice is meant to be, first and foremost, that of Christine de Pizan.

—Nadia Margolis
Amherst, Massachusetts, 1991

*The Book of the
Duke of True Lovers*

Fig. 1

Here the Book of The Duke of True Lovers begins.

Although my desire and inclination may not have been to compose tales of love right away, since I was pursuing another interest which gave me more pleasure, I want to begin a new poem now, in consideration of others' concerns. For someone who can easily command a far more important person than myself has asked me to do so. He is a lord I am bound to obey, who has graciously confessed to me the pain he has had for a long time, many a summer and winter, whether rightly or foolishly, because of Love, to whose service his heart remains pledged. But he does not want me to state his name: he is content to be called the Duke of True Lovers, the person who relates this tale for them. He is pleased to have me recount, just as he tells me, his woeful troubles and his joys, the things he has done, and the strange roads he has traveled for many years now. He asks that in this season of renewal a new story be told by me, and I agree. For I know him to be of good sense—the sort of person whose humility will take in good part the frailty of my small understanding. With his approval, I shall in his stead recount the facts of the matter as he expresses them. (41)

The Duke of True Lovers

I was young and much the child when I first set my efforts

toward becoming a lover. Because I had heard lovers praised more than other people and considered more gracious and better-taught, I wanted to be one. Toward that end I was often drawn to places where I might find a lady to serve. But I remained thus without a sweetheart for a long time because—upon my soul!—I lacked the sense to choose one; though I was certainly disposed to finding someone, I couldn't determine how. My desire caused me to frequent many a lovely group, where I saw many a lady and maiden whose every beauty was manifest. But Childhood still held me in its grip, so that I could not alight in any one place, no matter whom I might have chosen. For a long time I remained happy, carefree, and cheerful. In that sweet state I cried out often to Love, speaking in the following manner, because the time seemed long to me: (70)

Rondeau

True God of Love, who are to lovers lord,
And you, Venus, goddess most amorous,
Please take my heart and make it over as
Fit to love, then I desire nothing more.

So that to bravery I'm drawn forward,
Provide me a lady and a mistress,
True God of Love, who are to lovers lord.

And grant me the grace my choice to accord
To one, given my youth and callowness,
Who'd repay me and my honor address,
For my desire for this brings these words for'rd;
True God of Love, who are to lovers lord,
And you, Venus, goddess most amorous.

I often spoke thus, because of the desire I held in view, so that True Love heard me, and was gladdened by my wish. I'll relate

Fig. 2

how Love first seized and took hold of my heart, and how he has not released it since. One day, seeking diversion, I and one of my kin, along with four of my gentlemen, set out on horseback. I hungered for the chase and, for entertainment, I had my huntsmen take along greyhounds and ferrets. Without lingering we went down a road I often travel. We hadn't gone very far before a wide path led us to a place where I knew rabbits were plentiful. Nearby there stands a strong castle—an exceedingly fine one, I can assure you, but I'll forgo revealing its name. A princess had come to that castle, someone held by all to be so good, beautiful, and well-bred that everyone respected her. We hadn't known of her presence but had gone there quite by chance. Her attendants were amusing themselves out of doors here and there: some were singing, others were casting the *barre*, still others stood exercising at the bar. As they did so, we drew toward them. When they saw us and realized who we were, they quickly raised their heads. After they had greeted us respectfully, they did not hang back, it seems to me. Rather, they went off in groups of two and three to see their mistress, and I don't believe they hid our arrival from her, for as soon as we reached the castle we indeed saw a large group of ladies coming to meet us. They greeted us graciously and we turned toward them immediately, returned their greeting, and bid them rise from their curtsey. A lady and a maiden were there, kin to the lady who was mistress of them all. I kissed the blond maiden in greeting, quite innocently and blamelessly, and the lady, too. My cousin and I escorted the esteemed maiden and the cultivated lady, and we entered the house thus. The mistress had already emerged from her chambers and stood nobly before us, neither haughty nor arrogant, but exactly as is appropriate to her high station and royal person, of which everyone speaks well. The moment we saw her we greeted her in the manner due, and she stepped briefly forward, clasped my hand in her ungloved one, embraced me, and said: "Fair cousin, I didn't know you were coming. Welcome! What singular path brings you here?" My cousin said: "Indeed, my Lady, we were out seeking amusement. We didn't know you were here. Chance brings us by, but God be praised for gracing us so courteously that we found you here, your manner so welcoming." The good and gracious Lady laughed, and said: "Well then, shall we amuse ourselves?" (179)

We descended into a green meadow and, walking beside her, I entered a very beautiful place. The Lady drew me to her right side to sit next to her (without further ado, great pillows of gold and silk were brought) under the shade of a willow. There the waters of a spring run clear and sparkling in a channel that had been carved with skill through the tender, green grass, under a leafy bower. She did not remain standing but rather sat down and I next to her. Far from us, next to the small spring, the others sat down in scattered groups. She struck up a conversation with me, for I wouldn't have known how to talk to her or anyone else, I still believe, because I was very young then. She began by inquiring about a trip from which I had recently returned: How were the comportment and customs of the ladies in the place where I had been, and how was the court, held by a king and queen, governed? I answered her as I could, according to what I knew. We talked together of many things, as I recall. (213)

But now the time has come for me to relate how the painful malady began which, because I was in love, caused me to endure many bitter moments. It is astonishing to think how Love was able to take my heart away by means of her whom I'd seen a hundred times but had never, in all my young life, thought about before. Thus was I like the man who voyages across the sea, searching in many a distant land for what he can find close by but doesn't perceive until another makes him aware of it. That's exactly how it happened to me, without a doubt, for in my foolishness I had scarcely noticed my worthy Lady's beauty until Love pointed me toward it; then I desired to see only one like her so I could give her my heart. I often used to see her for long periods of time but, except for that day, I had paid no attention. Here I was holding in my hand the thing I had gone looking for

Fig. 3

elsewhere! Indeed, Love wanted to bring me peace from that strife, to soothe me in my youth. (243)

For at that moment as the perfect one who has caused me much pain spoke to me, her conversation and her sweet and genteel bearing pleased me more than ever before, and I was struck dumb. I looked at her with desire, studying her beauty, for she seemed more especially beautiful now than ever before, and possessed of much more elegance and far greater sweetness. Then Love, the playful archer, who saw my silent demeanor, and saw that I was ready to receive the arrow with which he's accustomed to taking lovers, took up his bow and stretched it taut, shooting without a sound. I didn't notice a thing. The arrow of Sweet Look, which is so pleasing and bountiful, pierced my heart through. Then was I bewildered! I thought I was lost when I felt the loving shot! But my heart consented to Love's wound. It did not bring death— rather, with that puncture my adventure began. (275)

Then her gently mirthful eyes, casting wide their nets of love, came to summon my heart, using such means that I could not answer when she spoke. She must have thought my manner and conduct foolish, for I often changed color when she looked at me and I moved neither hand nor foot, so that you might have thought my heart was trembling with fear. In brief, what shall I say? If I desired to be captured, I had not failed at my aim. And so my earliest youth came to an end. At that moment True Love taught me how to live differently; that was the hour of my capture. I lingered a while and, in an oafish way, like a great child, I talked on and ceaselessly fanned the spark burning in my heart by looking at her beauty. Just as the moth to the candle or the small bird in lime are caught, so I was caught; nor did I take heed. (305)

When I had been there nearly a third of a summer's day, my cousin wanted to depart. He said to me: "Take your leave. It is late and I fear, upon my soul, that you are keeping my Lady here too long. It is time for her to dine." The noble, courteous Lady, whom they call good and beautiful, pressed me earnestly to dine with her, but I excused myself and scarcely dallied there longer. I arose and tried to beg my leave, but first we were obliged to await the wine. We drank, and when we had drunk and eaten, I beseeched her to allow me, of her grace, to escort her back to her lodgings, but the beautiful creature refused. So I took my leave of her and of all the other ladies without lingering further. Then Love—just to make my tender heart burn the more—caused me to receive a sweet look from her as she came to see me off. For, in leaving, I turned my gaze upon her face; as I turned, she shot at me a gentle, delicious spark from her fair and loving eyes in such a way that the love that entered me has never left. And at that, I departed, bearing with me the arrow of love. (342)

When we were outside the castle parapets we mounted our horses straightaway and made haste to travel because of the approaching night. My cousin tried hard to make conversation, but as for me, I uttered not a sound as we went along. Rather, I remained quiet, and bowed my head, deep in thought. The quick, hot flame that Sweet Look had shot into my heart and attached there firmly didn't leave me. I was thinking constantly, unceasingly, about the beauties of that winsome face to which I had pledged my heart, and of the Lady's noble, shapely form, and her alluring eyes—all that swam before me. I went riding along, lost in thought. In the course of the trip, my cousin addressed me many a time upon many a subject, but I didn't hear him, for I was intent upon my revery. At last he said to me: "Fair sir, what are you thinking, without speaking, and why? Didn't you have enough happiness back there, you who are so pensive? For if God help me, I think that one couldn't wish for a more beautiful or perfect Lady, certainly, than the one you have just left. What do you say to that? Am I lying even a bit? Isn't she courteous and polished? Have you ever in all your life seen a Lady who was more perfect in every way? As far as I'm concerned, her beauty was made to be admired, and she surpasses all others especially in her good sense, honor, grace, and nobility. To say it all: by my soul, I have never seen her equal except for my Lady, mistress of my heart. For honor's majesty embellishes her noble heart, so that no other compares with her, except for the Lady I have mentioned, who is chosen among all ladies. It was she whom God wished to endow with that honor." (398)

When I heard another praised more than the Lady who was the object of my thoughts, although I had held my tongue until that moment, not for all the gold in the world would I continue to remain quiet! I sighed a sigh that came from my deepest thoughts, and said: "I'll give my opinion, indeed: if God wanted to choose a mistress and sweetheart on Earth, I don't believe it would be necessary to seek any other to have the most sovereign in the world, that is certain! And I would pledge myself in combat; if you do not take up this challenge, then you do not love that same Lady of yours, she who is without peer in the world! For no other comes close to my Lady—and don't say so anymore—no more than sparks, or candlelight, can rival the light of the stars!" (421)

When my cousin heard me talking that way, he smiled to himself secretly, and indeed I believe that he already noticed where my heart was directed. We let the matter drop and, by riding hard, we soon came to my residence. Deep night had fallen. Milord my father was above the courtyard, asking insistently where I had gone that day. And I, who was pressing forward hurriedly because I feared him and dreaded his anger, saw him at his window. Oh how I wished he were elsewhere! Nevertheless I got off my horse and greeted him right away on bended knee. Then he said, shaking his head: "Now where are you coming from, fair sir? Is the fall of night the moment to return home? But indeed, he fares well who fares forth and returns." (447)

I said not two words in reply. He left me and I went to my chamber. I dined in a reflective and somber mood, even though I had several young people about who tried to amuse me and tell me many a tale. But know that my thoughts were incessantly elsewhere, for I continued to imagine I could see, face to face, the Lady who did not know how she had captured my heart. (461)

When it was time to go to sleep I got into a rich and finely-
appointed bed, but I don't believe I slept for even an hour and
a half. One thing alone was weighing upon my mind: I feared
that chance would not let me see, as I might want to, the one
for whom I felt the sweet and agreeable sting. For I could not
choose another pleasure in all the world that might gratify me
as much as seeing her, nor one that would give my heart more
joy, as it seemed to me. I pondered it thus, and so thinking I
said: (477)

Ballade

Love, I surely find myself at a loss
To thank you enough for the gift of grace
You've sent me on the path of true love's cause,
And for the Lady whose surpassing ways
You've given me, for in beauty and grace
She's of sovereign worth, the truth to tell.
So I can't say enough nor might I pause:
My thanks to you who made me choose her well!

Now have I what I've desired at all cost:
To have a Lady with whom I could place
My service, my time, the most joyous thoughts
My heart could hold; through whom, in every space
I'd be jolly and gay, obey Love's laws
With all my heart; now my desire I quell.
I've chosen her, but Love, you've named the place,
My thanks to you, who made me choose her well!

I beg you, Love, to whom I'm at a loss,
To endow me with grace that I may face
Serving her so well that she'd still have cause
To see I'm all hers, and that her sweet face
And its gaze, which all my ills can efface,

Gently, through pity, upon me might dwell;
No more I ask of her, who has no flaws.
My thanks to you, who made me choose her well!

Ah, God of Love, before I end my days,
Grant that I might suffice and thus compel
Her to see I'm her sole friend to embrace.
My thanks to you, who made me choose her well!

That is how I reasoned with myself. I did not yet feel the fierce
assault of burning desire, which assails lovers, making them tremble and burn, grow pale, thirst, and become agitated. That had
not yet come to pass. For at that time I thought only of how I
would be elegant and dashing, how I would have a beautiful
mount and expensive clothing, and how, avoiding stinginess, I
would share my wealth generously. I would conduct myself so
honorably that, in sum, the report of noblemen would praise me
everywhere, with the result that my Lady would let me into her
graces because of the good I was doing. Thus I wanted to perfect
my comportment, from then on leaving behind me the childhood
that hitherto had kept me foolish. I would never let a fickle
thought seize me, and I wanted my heart to learn the right road
toward becoming more valorous. I had all those intentions then,
and I sought the way, through deed and bearing, to put them
all into effect. So I indeed changed my manner, for my entire
intent was but to think, say, and do things that in every instance
might be charming and gracious, and on no account would I do
anything ungracious. For that reason I was never sad or silly, but
cheerful, well-groomed, happy and joyful. In order to acquire
the ways of love I took pains to learn how to sing and dance, and
to take up arms. I thought that by pursuing love, arms, and
valor, honor surely would come, and so it truly does. (554)
Without delaying, then, I pursued every possible means before
my father and my mother so that I obtained what I was after: I
would have gold and silver for the great disbursements I would

make, and would be richly clothed in every way. I selected an emblem and an appropriate motto in which my Lady's name occurred in such a way that no one could recognize it. I wanted to have chargers for jousting, and I undertook to have a festival prepared in which I could learn to joust—or so I said, but I had something else in mind. And thus the celebration was held to which many an estimable lady was bidden. But well before I knew whether my Lady would come to our festival, I made request of an appropriate person, someone distantly related to me, who indeed granted it gladly and received me at his residence. There I saw my Lady at my leisure but did not tell her how I loved her with body and soul, and cherished her. I think my face made it sufficiently plain though, for Love, who was using all his tricks on me—the better to smite me—made me grow pale and then regain my color, changing completely. But my fair one said nothing about this, as if she had not noticed. I don't think she knew so little, though, that she failed to understand the reason for everything happening to me: that it came entirely from love, of which she was the cause and source of the loving spark that struck my heart, which hardly complained! I lived in happiness, however, and saw her often. That comforted my heart, which rejoiced, and in the manner of an aside to myself, I spoke as follows to my Lady: (607)

Ballade

My sovereign Lady, rare flower on high;
Goddess of all honor and worthiness;
Fountain of beauty, sense and kind reply;
And who to me points the path and access
To gain valiance; and to whom I address
All my deeds; Lady, I'm pledged to obey,
As the humblest serf to his good mistress,
To serve you for all of my mortal stay.

•

With this I must, sweet lovely one, comply,
For you surpass all, and your loftiness
Will be my model; and now lead me nigh
To portals of honor and happiness.
And for your sweet pleasure I cannot rest
From being glad, my Lady—thus essay
In body and soul, despite lowliness,
To serve you for all of my mortal stay.

You'll see that on me you'll surely rely—
When the time comes, most high, noble duchess—
On how much my heart, to serve you, will try.
I'll then measure up in complete fullness
When you note that, each day, without slackness,
From my soul's pith and branches, I'll obey,
With conduct honorable and valorous,
To serve you for all of my mortal stay.

Exalted, powerful, much-praised princess!
To love you I mastered from the first day;
Improved am I—I'll do my humble best,
To serve you for all of my mortal stay.

But now I must return to my principal subject. Preparations for the grand and lovely festival, at which many people amused themselves, were hurried along. The jousts were proclaimed: he who won the jousting would receive a jewel of great worth, and thus the prize, and there would be twenty capable knights who would joust with all the *venans*. The day for the gathering was set, and it would take place in a fair meadow, where there is a castle with six towers overlooking a pond. In the fields tents were set up, and high and wide scaffolding and pavilions were erected, and all the arrangements were made for the festival and the jousting. Now, without adding further detail, I tell you that when the day came that we had planned, my Lady arrived toward evening. I set out to meet her with a fine company of noble people. There were, to be sure, more than three pairs of minstrels, trumpets, and drums; they blew so loudly that the hills and valleys resounded. (669)

You understand that I was filled with joy when I saw my goddess come to my house. Nothing else could have happened to me that would have given me such joy. As I met her along the way with a very noble retinue, I approached her litter and greeted her, and she me. My beautiful Lady said to me: "You are giving yourself a great deal of trouble, my friend, coming here now. There is no need to." Thus with me talking happily to my sweet, dear Lady of one thing and another, we approached the castle. Riding next to her litter I certainly had enough of a reward for my trouble, I thought, because my great joy doubled when I perceived her behaving toward me in a friendlier fashion than ever before. We arrived at the castle where we found a fine group of ladies who curtsied before her in the manner due her station. She entered the courtyard, alighted from the litter, and was received with great joy. At her side, I guided her through the house into the changing rooms. My father, upon whom I depended and whose property I would inherit, had had all the lodgings decorated. (707)

Then the wine and sweets were brought by the bearers and the fair one invited me to partake of them with her. After that, my party withdrew and went elsewhere, allowing the Lady her privacy. I went off to another room on the right, where I dressed, attiring myself to dance the Allemande. So that the festival would lack nothing to make it perfect, I had had a hundred rich liveries made to my design. I believe that twenty-five of them—the knights wore them—were made of green velvet with appliqués in hammered gold cloth. The next day, after the joust, the squires and gentlemen (certainly not the servitors) put on satin that had been embroidered in silver with no thought to cost. When we were dressed, we went to my Lady. There we found a great throng of noble ladies and married women and maidens from the countryside, who had come to the festival. Immediately I greeted my Lady, as well as all the others, and I'm sure I blushed. I said: "My Lady, it is time for the evening meal." Then, without waiting, I took her arm and led her into the dining hall. The others followed. Knights escorted ladies, and those minstrels trumpeted so that the sound rang out, lending luster to the festival, which was very lovely to see! I seated my Lady in a prominent position at the high table; I don't think it displeased her! Next I seated my mother, quite near to her. Four countesses sat after her, who took their places rightfully. And in order, throughout the hall, each according to her rank, the noble ladies were seated, and the gentlemen sat alongside. In sum, I believe that all were copiously served with meats and wines at supper—I'm not guessing at that. Now without lingering here on the details, I'll simply tell you that when we had finished eating, after the sweets, we drank, and then minstrels came forward and began to trumpet in gracious harmony. Soon the latest dance began, joyful and gay, and every man was happy, looking at the handsome celebration. (776)

At that I hung back no longer, instead going straightaway to invite my Lady to dance. She demurred a bit but did not refuse me. I took her by the arm and led her to the dance, then back to her place—and there can be no doubt I was so head over heels in love that I felt transported by joy at being near her. I would have abandoned heavenly Paradise for this, I believe, nor could I have asked for better. What charmed and gladdened me more was her very sweet face which bore no sign of reticence or refusal, but was so pleasant, and appeared so favorable toward me through the amiable offices of Sweet Look, that I believed she viewed with approval all that I said and did. I saw it in her actions, and I cried out for the great joy I felt, so that it seemed I would fly! It was fitting for me to approach her gaily. (806)

And thus, pleasurably, we had danced a great part of the night away when the party ended. It was time to retire and the beds were readied. Then I escorted the Lady, blond as amber, to her room. We exchanged many a gracious word and, after her eyes had gazed on me—the better to set me aflame—and after partaking of the sweets, I took leave of her and of all the ladies. In fine beds, under rich covers, we retired in our various places. But I didn't stop thinking all night about the beauty that was hers! I pronounced these words, which I read in my thoughts: (825)

Rondeau

My heart rejoices at your coming here
So much that for you in pure joy it leaps;
Flow'r of beauty, Rose that in freshness steeps,
To whom I'm a serf, and sweetly adhere.

Lovely Lady and one whom all revere
As best of all, for her beauty so deep;
My heart rejoices at your coming here.

Because of you the feast will persevere
In great revelry; no one such joy reaps
Within me but you, who alone appear
The one for whom life all joy in me keeps;
My heart rejoices at your coming here
So much that for you in pure joy it leaps.

In the morning, like one burning with love, I was already longing to see my Lady. I got out of bed the moment I saw it was time. The house was already full of brave and valorous knights and squires jousting with blunted tips, often bringing each other down. When I was ready and mass had been said, I went out, but because I hadn't seen my Lady I became pensive. I set out to find her and came upon her newly up and refreshed and already at mass; she was hurrying to hear it so as to prepare her attire. Her handsome person impressed everyone, in truth. As she left the chapel I greeted her courteously, and she said lovingly: "Fair cousin, welcome! You have many a task ahead, and he who will have a beautiful lady will become known at the joust!" (865)

I began to smile and found the courage to say: "My Lady, I wish to make a request of you, and if you are willing to grant it, I will be very happy. It is that it may please you to give me the sleeve of one of your bodices and a periwinkle chaplet to wear upon my helmet. Were you to give me a kingdom, I don't believe I would love it more, nor would I be more joyful." My Lady thought a bit and then said: "Fair cousin, certainly it would be better for you to have a gift for your services from another lady for whom you would soon perform chivalrous and noble deeds. Many a lady of distinction has come here and it isn't possible that you won't find a lady, and without risk to anyone—it's good to know that. It is from her that you must have a gift to place upon the crest of your helmet, for whom you must engage in deeds of chivalry. Let your effort be rewarded by your lady and friend, not by me. Mind you, I'm not saying that I might refuse your request or submit to the grief of doing so. I would do more for you, but I don't want anyone to know it." (900)

Then she herself seized a knife from behind her drapes and she cut the ermine and gold sleeve of one of her bodices and gave it to me, for which I thanked her heartily. Later I received from her the verdant chaplet, about which I was happy and gay. I said I would wear it on my crest and that I would joust for her love, and that she should take it all in good part, for I still had to learn how. My well-bred Lady grew silent and gave no sign of whether this pleased or displeased her, and I no longer dared to speak. (918)

I took my leave, for it was time to go. Our meal was prepared early that day and we all dined briefly in our chambers. Then we went out to the fields where the jousts were to take place. We proceeded over the field to the handsome pavilions that were erected. The equipment was already there, the lances were being readied, and the chargers were being put through their paces.

You would have seen high saddles with stirrups, white, red, and green, and covered with devices, shields of many colors, and painted lances. There was a great deal of equipment, much noise, and the sound of many voices. There were people in many a selion. In my tent I armed and readied myself, but I lingered there a while since it was not appropriate for me to lead off the jousting. We were twenty in our unit and all outfitted alike, and we were all knights, who would joust with those from outside. (947)

My cousin, about whom I spoke above, who had abundant goodness, was the first on the field. He was quite accustomed to that. He entered in such magnificent display, in complete regalia, that he seemed kin to a king: his helmet laced on, he himself outfitted beautifully, with banner and painted lances, and with a very handsome company. You could have seen and heard many a piper around there spreading cheer about. But we'll talk no more of that. I had had many tents set up there awaiting those from outside, where they could stay and shelter themselves. Believe me that before the day was out many valorous gentlemen came there, who gave us a good match in the joust. Others, who came to observe, sat on horseback. (973)

Without waiting long my cousin found his joust with a knight who aimed his lance at him, but my cousin didn't turn away. He met him and in the encounter knocked him from his horse so soundly that blood must have been spilled. We had won the *commençaille!* At that you would have heard the heralds cry and loudly call out his name, which was known in England and many a land. Then from the tent five of our men issued forth; they did not fail to find a challenger. Each one of them, in truth, did his duty so very well that he should be renowned for his deeds. The jousting over the fields began now high and low. In double file and strongly reinforced, our men went forth and, as they should, they jousted boldly. Then the minstrels trumpeted gaily and the heralds cried out, and those knights jousted enthusiastically throughout the different ranks, on great and eager chargers. (1003)

Fig. 4

My Lady and many another, pictures of beauty, were in the richly-draped spectators' galleries, graduated by many steps, the high-born ladies wearing crowns. They were twenty ladies with blond tresses whose sovereign and mistress was the Lady on my mind. All twenty ladies, for sure, were garbed in white silk with a device embroidered in gold—they seemed like goddesses come from Heaven, or fairies, made exactly as one might wish, all perfect. You may be sure that they inspired many clear exploits during that day. The scene could not have given only small pleasure to those who looked upon such creatures, so the combattants made great efforts to increase their worth and to outshine one another to earn the ladies' favor. There you might have seen many blows struck in different ways, and how one struck and unseated the other, and how the next, with another sort of stroke, aimed at the visor eye slits, or struck shield or helmet, the one unhelmeting the other, or bringing him down in a heap, and then another came along who removed him from the field. Lances broke, blows resounded, and those minstrels trumpeted loudly, so that God thundering might not have been heard. And thus, one against the other, they delivered great blows on both sides. (1042)

At that point I left my tent, my lance at rest, happier than a merlin, firmly in the stirrups, armed all in white on a white-caparisoned charger, with no other color—no red, no green—but fine gold. All who were in the pavilion issued forth and struck many a fine blow. Our men were armed all in white, and the lances they bore were of no color but white. I had ordered the richly-designed sleeve given me by my Lady to be attached securely to my crest so that no one might tear it off, and on my helmet the green chaplet. With a good company of men, I set out, for I was yearning to see my very winsome goddess. I arrived where the jousting was, filled with joy. I raised my eyes to where she was and received her sweet look, and so had no thought of any harm. I passed in review before her, then quickly helmeted myself and withdrew to the ranks. (1074)

At once, in my Lady's view, a noble count gave me my lance, saying that it would be a great dishonor if I didn't joust well when I had such a noble crest! With my lance lowered, and wishing it to be well-positioned, I spurred my charger without restraint against another. You could have seen him come toward me, and we didn't falter in the encounter! But since it's embarrassing to tell of one's own deeds, I would not like to continue in this vein, except to say that my noble Lady thought my feats that day so well done that she gave me very great praise (thanks be to her!) and in the end she gave me the prize for the defenders. I took it, with the kind agreement of her ladies, and I was thoroughly jubilant. Know surely that all day long, to my ability, I did my duty as my young years allowed. If I performed deeds of prowess there, no praise is mine, for it can be said that Love did it all, not I, and one mustn't make anything of it. There's no doubt that Love had found many experienced knights in that group, much better than me, for men of high and lesser station had come from everywhere and had better earned the prize—they knew it well. But I believe that the ladies chose me because they saw how fervent I was. That's why I think that in giving me the prize they took good will for accomplished fact, so that I would more willingly enter jousts. The prize announced for the challengers was given to a skillful German, a powerful jouster among a thousand. (1125)

Thus the jousting lasted all that day. New challengers appeared continuously and our men jousted against all comers. What should I say, in sum? All did fine and well, but there is no need for me to describe all the blows they struck—who, what, how, and in what style—for that's beside my point, nor is it what I propose to report. Night came, the jousting subsided. All the men and women left and returned to the castle, where the cooks were hurrying supper. (1142)

I sent my gentlemen to the outside lodgings, on behalf of the worthy ladies and myself, to beseech both the foreign gentlemen and those of my acquaintance, as I would friends, and as many as I could, to come and join us in celebrating. Thus I had a Round Table announced all about so that whoever wished would come and keep the feast. From the greatest to the least they came, with none remaining outside. And so barons from many countries were there—no need to ask whether the assembly was large, for so many people were welcomed with enormous joy that the castle was filled. I received them gladly. There was a great throng of knights and of gentlemen from many a land, and I honored each expressly and according to his rank. The meal was copious and memorable. When we arose from the table, minstrels trumpeted and noble partners drew themselves up for dancing. There wasn't one who didn't have on clothing richly embroidered with gold and silver work in great bands, and you would have seen ladies all dressed alike, in the same liveried attire. They readied themselves to dance elegantly. You would have seen a joyous ball begin happily, where many a gracious, noble lady and demoiselle courteously sought out the foreign guests and invited them to dance, leading them away. You would have seen round dances progressing through the hall, each guest striving to dance gaily. (1192)

And I, in whom Love had kindled the flame of desire, had no thought, glance, or wish but for my Lady. I delayed dancing a bit so that no one would perceive or know my thoughts. Rather, I remained with the knights who were not dancing until messengers came to tell me that I should go into the ballroom without delay, for my Lady was sending for me, asking for me in great earnest. I was certainly happy about that! With a fine company of gentlemen I entered the room, where no one was sad but rather all were vying with each other at dancing. When I reached my Lady, she said, "Fair cousin, why aren't you dancing?" I replied, "Come, my Lady, and dance with me, and show me the way!" (1215)

She said that I should dance first with another. And so to begin, I led a pretty lady cheerfully onto the floor. I danced her around once or twice, then escorted her back to her place. Then I took my Lady by the hand and led her to the dance happily, with her consent. The dancing lasted thus the greater part of that night and later was dispersed. Each guest retired, to lie down between fine white linens. (1229)

But I, who had a lady and mistress, and who felt in my breast the distress of my desire to be loved by her, by which I was pierced through, said to myself:

Rondeau

Laughing gray eyes, whose impression I bear
Within my heart in pleasant memory,
How this flash of memory gladdens me
About you, sweet one, who hold me in fear.

Love's sickness caused my life to disappear,
And yet you sustain the vigor in me,
Laughing gray eyes, whose impression I bear.

To me you're the goal of all that's dear,
Hence I'll come to where I desire to be:
T'is retained as her serf Madame wants me
To be; I'll be held by you so near,
Laughing gray eyes, whose impression I bear
Within my heart in pleasant memory.

Day came, and what should I say? Why would I prolong my subject without reason? The next day squires jousted almost the entire day, who deported themselves well in every way. There were twenty, dressed in green and bearing a device, who won the day, and the ladies came to observe them and to bestow the prize. There were twenty young ladies dressed in green who had golden chaplets in their hair, and all were very great ladies, noble and beautiful. Because of them many chargers with high saddles were brought down in encounters that day, and there was much striking of shields and breaking of lances. There one saw many a praiseworthy blow given and received. But I don't want to continue making a long account of that, for it pleases me more to talk about what I began this story for, and what I thought, did, and said in this love, about which I've since uttered many a plaint. (1278)

The pleasant festival lasted three whole days—that's no invention—at which all were welcome and took their ease. Then the feast dispersed, but my Lady did not leave the place for another whole month. I beseeched him who was master to grant that month's stay, which he did, and for that I would willingly have paid him rent, had I dared! You can understand the joy I must have had in that pleasant stay. I never thought of anything but of how I might best entertain her. One day I ordered baths and had the water heated and the tubs placed in an attractive spot inside white pavilions. I had to go there just when my Lady was in the bath, which didn't sadden me a bit! Rather, my joy was complete when I saw her form and her skin as white as the lily flower. That gave me great delight, as you can fully imagine, you who hear this being told! (1310)

One day we went game hunting, another we rode down to the river to hunt for birds. In that way, taking many a happy path, we passed that entire month. (1316)

But you should know that in my pleasure Love tightened his nets around my heart more than ever before and held my heart so tightly that a great desire to be loved burned in me. By the time the revelry ended, no harsher tempest had been suffered by any other poor man. My only pleasure was in seeing her, my eyes gazing steadily upon her, which I might never tire of doing, nor did I think I could ever have had enough of her company. Sweet Wishing made me desire the relief of being with her, so much that I couldn't avoid grieving deeply. I wasn't clever enough, believe me surely, to hide the great pain that I bore, even though I did not wish to open my mind to a living man or woman. So driven was I, and so carried away, that my appearance showed how I felt, in spite of what I might suffer as a result. I couldn't avoid being now deep in reverie, now quite awake, generally behaving like a man gone astray. I often wept so much that I thought I was dying of great grief, despairing and lacking any hope of ever obtaining her love. I couldn't help growing pale, quivering, turning red, and changing color often, and sweating, trembling, then shivering. Consequently, my heart sometimes gave out completely and I would take to my bed very often without uttering a word. I didn't drink or taste the flavor of any nourishment, nor could I sleep for anything. I became so over-wrought that I grew much the worse. No one knew what was wrong with me, for in no way did I want to talk about myself to anyone, nor would I have confessed my situation on pain of death, not even to her whom I loved. And, nevertheless, she often inquired of me what was wrong, and begged me to tell her and not to hide my state, and to speak to her without fear, for I should not doubt that she would make every effort to pull me out of it. Thus, over a long period of time, my Lady comforted me, but I wouldn't have dared reveal or confess for all the gold in the world the burden my heart carried. So I wept and sighed from deep within my thoughts. I don't know what else I could say about it. I came to know Desire then, but my introduction to him was hard and painful, for since that time the peaceable, happy joy disappeared that I had had before, and my heart leapt into another prison. All happiness had to become a stranger to me as Sadness had to become my Hostess. I spent a long time in that state without daring to ask for mercy, out of fear of rejection. So, sorrowing, I said these words, lamenting my pain: (1404)

Ballade

Love, may I never presume
You'd for your servant obtain
Such suff'ring as all consumes,
For more I cannot sustain.

On the saints I'll swear again
That 'til my death, days are few
If I've not some help from you.

For ardent Desire does doom
Me such that I can't remain
With the pain he's caused to loom.
It's up to you: please contain
My suff'ring and me maintain;
No other cure's in view,
If I've not some help from you.

I would rather death assume,
I swear to you, than sustain
That long suff'ring heap its gloom,
Pent-up ardor to restrain
In my heart; I thus refrain
From speech. Decline is my due
If I've not some help from you.

Love, through joy I wish to strain
Evil, a pure heart to gain.
So 'tis pain that will ensue
If I've not some help from you.

At the end of the month my Lady, for whom I lived in a state
of urgent desire, was required to leave the aforementioned manor;
she could not stay longer, so she departed. I was in a bad way
about that because I was losing the sight of the very exquisite,
beautiful woman without whom I could not live. I was entirely
deprived of joy, since for a long time I had been used to seeing
her and being with her. But now it would be necessary to go
without hearing news of her or seeing her for three or four months
(the possibility of such a long separation loomed ahead), which
was a very harsh thing for me to endure. I was nostalgic for the

Fig. 5

time we'd spent together and felt such sadness at this departure that I lost color, reason, composure, and countenance. I believe (it could well have been) that many people noticed the state I was in, about which they exchanged gossip that was taken seriously. My chagrin was so great at hearing the rumor fly, about how I loved my beautiful Lady, that I thought I would die of grief. My pain grew worse, for I feared the talk would put an end to the great friendship between myself and her friends. That sad thought gave me very disagreeable pain, for I feared she was being made to leave because of the gossip. So displeased was I that I couldn't express it. Nevertheless I hid my painful anguish to the best of my ability and even better than was my wont, and sighing, burdened with grief, I uttered these words: (1475)

Ballade

Now from all things my joy's but nothingness,
And my solace to bitterness changed face.
My sweetest flower, since our separateness
I've gone far from you, and your gentle ways
    That used to be—
When I'd see you every day, you whose glee
Sustained me—exchanged for raw misery.
Alas! How can I now bid you good-bye?

My sweet love, my Lady, my share in bliss,
The one for whom my inner desires blaze,
What shall I do when in neither all nor less
I receive from Love naught but froth and haze?
    Where'er I be
I'll have neither comfort nor gaiety
From your beauty afar, no more close by.
Alas! How can I now bid you good-bye?

Vile gossips! You've wrought this work from malice,

And my death you've forged on an anvil's space.
Fortune's consented to my cruel duress,
Yields neither my body nor pen a place.
     No way is free
Save for death. I pray God for company,
Since without you none other would I try.
Alas! How can I now bid you good-bye?

     Ah, plainly, calmly,
Standing there; at least deign my tears to see
As you depart, which I'm tormented by.
Alas! How can I now bid you good-bye?

The day of leave-taking came and my Lady departed. I believe
that she would have refrained from going had she dared, but she
had to obey. And so, as was befitting her noble and well-bred
disposition, she thanked everyone, begged her leave, and set out.
And I, who escorted her, rode next to her litter. The fair one,
who could wholly perceive that I loved her truly without deception, looked at me in serious concern, with such sweet demeanor
that I believe she wanted to comfort my weak and grieving heart.
She might have said more to me, but on her left rode another
who came so close that we hadn't the chance to say anything for
which he could have reproached us, because of which I hated him
profoundly. But I saw that I would have to suffer many dangers;
that would happen often. Thus we rode until, in a day and a
half, we reached her dwelling. The trip did not seem long to me,
however—rather, it seemed to pass quickly—for I hadn't tired
of it, though I was truly suffering. I thought to take leave of her,
but the master, feigning welcome, endeavored to keep me there,
and I knew, from his behavior, that he was frantic because of me.
Someone who was at our revel had put this jealousy in his mind.
(I have since given that man his due, but I waited until no one
was paying attention.) Thus this evil man watched the fair one,
whom I adored, and, because of that, I was dying of grief. I took

my leave and set off, dissimulating and hiding my misery, nor did I raise my eyes to look at my sovereign Lady, which was a tormenting pain. My heart could barely restrain itself, as it had to, for fear of the scandalmonger. And so I said: (1565)

Ballade

Farewell, my Lady I dread;
Farewell, queen of all who reign;
Farewell, perfect in blameless stead,
Farewell, noblest, of honor plain;
Farewell, faithful to ascertain;
Farewell, flow'r cherished everywhere;
Farewell not farewell, blond and fair.

Farewell, wise one on whom none tread;
Farewell, stream with joy in its train;
Farewell, noble fame's watershed;
Farewell, songbird of sweet refrain;
Farewell, sweet payment for my pain;
Farewell, you who all graces bear;
Farewell not farewell, blond and fair.

Farewell, sweet eyes that through me read;
Farewell, looks Helen can't attain;
Farewell, by soul and senses led;
Farewell, most gracious in demesne;
Farewell, North Star, our joyous vane;
Farewell, wave of valuable fare;
Farewell not farewell, blond and fair.

Farewell, princess of high domain;
Farewell, whose smile brings fear in train;
Farewell, you who all vice forswear;
Farewell not farewell, blond and fair.

Thus I spoke to myself and went along sighing, and by dint of effort I arrived at my manor. I felt myself invaded by grief and dismay when I did not see her there whom I had chosen as my Lady, whom my heart held so very dear! (1599)

Thus far I have related how I first desired to be in love, and how in that sweet state Love wounded me with the dart from which my heart will never regain its health. Now I will tell about the pain that since then I have endured, but it's also right that I tell of the good things. That illness multiplied and grew, which caused my vigor to decline, so that I became pale, thin, and weak. Often, alas, I recited poems in my misery, for, unable to find any way to see my sweet Lady, I had no source of comfort. I so feared her blame that I didn't dare approach her, despite my inner conflict. That caused me to dissolve in tears and destroyed me. I uttered this ballade: (1624)

Ballade

Since your sovereign beauty I can behold
No more, my love, Lady, sole joy profound,
My heart's mortal suff'ring has taken hold.
For were I to have worldly wealth abound,
Without seeing you, I'd have nothing found;
So far from you, I need lodge my complaint,
Missing good things that I'd easily found;
So to no one but you could I lament.

For, true love, this you may surely uphold:
My mem'ry's vision of you does resound,
Never to leave, within me to unfold
Your beauty before me, calm and uncrowned,
For which Desire to make war seems so bound
Against my poor heart, that I feel it spent,
In death I'd be from this illness unbound;
So to no one but you could I lament.

·

Alas! At least, fair one, whom in pain I behold,
If I die for you—for that path I've found—
Pray for me, my soul's welfare to uphold.
And if your sweet eyes a few tears shed round,
My soul will be glad of this; if it found
That my pain makes you in pity relent—
Moan just a bit—for you in tears I'm drowned,
So to no one but you could I lament.

Ah, sweet flower, to whom by oath I'm bound,
Now I feel my heart's too bitterly pent
And Fortune on our reunion has frowned.
So to no one but you could I lament.

That pain lasted for some time, during which my heart endured
a very grievous burning desire. Such harsh pain would have led
me to my death without fail if God had not soon brought to me
the kinsman mentioned earlier, my guarantee against death. He
came from abroad, and he fully perceived and recognized the ill
that constrained me. He found me very sick, my color drained
and dull, and that weighed upon him grievously. He came as
quickly as he could to talk to me. I was cheered as soon as I
heard his voice, for I loved him very dearly. He wept when he
saw me grown so much worse, and I drew him toward me,
embracing him for dear love. (1675)

He said to me: "Heavens, what sort of face is that, and is it
really as I see? I must know your state, certainly, with nothing
withheld. You mustn't hide your feelings from me nor your
situation, not any more than you would from a priest to whom
you make confession. You would surely be a great fool to keep
enclosed in your heart the pain that holds your happiness and
good health in its grip. I have been out in the world so much
that I see, recognize, and understand what's wrong with you, for
I have been tried by such torment. It isn't an illness but a passion,

Fig. 6   How the Lover laments to his companion

for it comes to you without fail from Love, who is burning you up as fire burns straw—you can't teach me anything about that! You would be doing wrong to our true friendship if you feared that I would reveal anything at all, or that I might not conceal what you tell me more than I would my own affairs. Tell me about the suffering that holds you so cruelly, the what and how of it, and you will find your miseries diminished, there's no doubt of it. For a man who suffers from lovesickness without talking about it with anyone does himself very great harm. So tell me all about your state, my gentle cousin, lord, and master, leaving nothing behind in your heart. If not, I'll return to Germany for a long time, for don't think that my grief is small at seeing you thus. It isn't the sort of thing that gives me pleasure." (1716)

When he who cherished me had, as best he knew how, exhorted me to reveal and tell all my thinking to him, his gentle speech so softened and captured my heart that I was seized by such sobbing and weeping that it seemed I was dying of grief. I could not have spoken to him then, even had he given me all the world. And he, because of the ill he saw me suffer, began to weep in great pity, chagrined and overwhelmed. He offered himself and his wealth earnestly to me to restore my happiness: he would make every effort, never was there greater; he would not fail at it, and would counsel me well; I should take comfort and cease weeping, for there was neither sense nor honor in it. (1741)

And thus my dear friend admonished me to cheer up. Then, without waiting, I said: "Gentle cousin and friend, I know well that you have great love for me, and so I do for you. We mustn't conceal from one another our joys and losses, nor other important experiences whatever. So I'll tell you all about me, I won't lie, although I've never spoken of it to a single person, however I might have loved that person. (1754)

"Very kind cousin, if you recall, a while ago you and I went to a place quite near here where we found that a lady had arrived whose visit I have since paid for dearly. For from that point my ignorant and carefree childhood was taken from me; and Love,

80

thinking to do no harm, made me love her because of whom I'm dying. But no one should blame me, for there is not another woman her equal in beauty, sense, or worth, without doubt. Now, you know how I undertook our celebration, which was splendid; it was done entirely for love of her. Later, when the revelry was over, I made request of the appropriate party to let my Lady remain all summer at our manor to amuse and enjoy herself by hunting in the forest, which was green and still is. Be advised that he granted it willingly; I think you didn't stay more than a week after that, for you soon departed. I remained in joy because I saw my Lady as I wished during this time. But Misfortune, who goes about furnishing many an ill to lovers, caused someone (let evil flames burn him!) to take notice of my demeanor in order to make me unhappy. Like a man filled with spite he indeed took note of me—I who was too much the novice—and of my feelings, and of how my heart was pledged to her alone. I have no idea how he could have perceived it, for in order to deceive everyone in the matter I took pains to conceal myself and I visited as many or more other ladies, nor did I tell a soul my thoughts—not even her whose liege I am. She knows nothing of this, which grieves me. That disloyal person made such noise about it, and such inquiry, that the Lady's jealous husband made her leave without staying further. If I hadn't feared bringing worse damage to her honor I would have made the man who caused this tremble and repent on pain of death, and feel my pain and sorrow. Thus in displeasure have I lived the last three months. I would have preferred dying to continuing to live in this way, just in order to be freed from this doleful pain, since I cannot otherwise see her—although she has since (thanks be to her!) asked after my condition and requested that, for a little a while, I refrain from seeing her and give no sign of anything. She said that a time would come when things would be otherwise and that I should maintain a sanguine demeanor. I know that my dear Lady recognizes and knows without doubt that I love her completely (at least I think so), but I cannot suffer lightly the strain of desire that I feel, because I long for her very much. I have seen her since, but not so that others would know, for I disguised myself in order not be recognized, and I saw her pass by from a distance. I have since had to spend my life thus, as you hear, in such grief that I haven't any desire except to die soon, if I do not see that you or another might help me. For it is impossible that the Lady's jealous husband or his watchmen do not notice it; and do not doubt that I must recover from this or die. You can hear how glad I am for this harsh acquaintance with Love, and how I upbraid him in my ballade! Listen; lean a bit closer: (1860)

Ballade

Ah, Love! Well you've betrayed me:
First, to trick me, seemed my friend
So kind, then my enemy
So cruel that my life I'd end
Through you! One must reprehend
Your two natures, slyly placed:
One, toward ashen hues does tend,
The other being angel-faced.

I, stunned in obscurity
Find myself, as I descend
Through Desire, who fearsomely
Struck me. Yet Despair does rend
My heart, and Hope does not bend
To my plight: one appears crazed
With rage, dark death to portend;
The other being angel-faced.

So I reaped Hope's enmity,
And with Desire you intend
To cause my death—"So sorry,"

You'd say gently to pretend;
In truth you your web extend,
Both Danger- and Welcome-graced:
One from Satan does descend,
The other being angel-faced.

Love, you've made me comprehend
That after joy can gloom subtend
One who has your honor praised.
You've two modes: one can scorn send,
While the other's angel-faced.

My cousin thought highly of that ballade but he was greatly
saddened by my trouble. And I, who do not tire of weeping and
never cease, then finished my explanation; my pain was lightened.
But my cousin grew angry because he saw me dejected and doing
nothing to divert myself. He said to me: "Come now! I know
that this way of behaving little suits you. What reason have you,
fair Sir, to conduct yourself in this way? Truly, you should be
happy, from what I've heard, when your Lady, through her messenger, promises you some recompense, in some place at some
time. You aren't clever when you lose hope, which comforts you.
Know that your Lady sees you love her, and she is eager to give
you pleasure. How can such affliction plant itself in your foolish
heart so that you retreat like this and kill yourself with despair?
Many lovers, without hope of being loved by their ladies, have
given long service, in great distress, without receiving any reward,
neither for talent nor wealth. They had not even a single glance
from their ladies, nor did they dare go where their ladies were,
for fear of scandal. So suffer and believe my words, for you have
nothing to complain about, according to what I've heard, and
you'll soon be able to attain your desire. Since your Lady views
your cause favorably, you have nothing to fear—there won't be
a guard strong enough to turn you away. But, however grievous
it may be, it could be foolishly destructive for you that you have

spent so long without telling her your situation. You understand that she will hardly come and ask you! And I don't know how you could have been so foolish when you were with her freely, without Danger, that, without pondering the matter interminably, you didn't tell her surely all the love you have for her." (1947)

"Alas, cousin, I would not have dared! Yes, I had enough opportunities indeed, but I was fearful and so very afraid of her that I wouldn't have said anything on pain of death, for which I sigh and repent greatly. I never had the boldness, for my heart trembled before her. And yet, when I was by myself, I thought that I would tell her. I often thought so, but of course I couldn't keep to it when I was with her! The pleasure of her loving glance, so very charming to me, made me so light-headed that I believed she noticed my suffering without being told." (1967)

Then my cousin answered me. "Foolish is the lover who hides and conceals from a Lady the love he has for her, for by my soul, the delay can hurt him very much. Since you didn't dare say it, for the fear you had, and since you certainly know how to write, why don't you put it in writing, in a missive, or other record? Indeed, I couldn't be any more astonished at your folly when, considering the time you've been separated from her, you didn't send back news of your state when you received her message! Why did you delay? For it came with sure intention. Childishness held you back, that's the truth. You can perceive, since she was willing for you to be given so much, that she was thinking about hearing some news of you, and that your love was on her mind. So she must believe you're a dolt for not sending any word to her! Never let a word touching your desolation issue from your mouth! Instead, let your heart rejoice, and let me handle matters. I'll be tonsured if there's a man alive—so much will I know how to blind them all to what's happening!—who might stand in the way of your seeing the fair one secretly and quietly, if both she and you want it. Now then, on your feet! Be sad no longer, and put on a glad face! For without lecturing you further, I promise and affirm to you that you will see your Lady more than once before the week is out. If God shows me how, I'll find the way." (2012)

Then, as light comes to illumine shadowy seasons and brilliant sunshine takes away darkness, the grievous hardship of my pain was healed and evaporated by my cousin, who comforted me so well that he gave me back joy and solace and made my sadness cease. I had nothing to complain about, and he was not negligent. Before he had been gone for an hour and a half, he set out to see my Lady. To tell it briefly, he spoke wisely to the fair one and procured every happiness for my relief. Speaking with the authority of a personal witness, he told the whole truth: how he had found me almost dead, and how he didn't know whether I could recover from the illness that kept me in bed in silence and chagrin. He told her everything, and said, in short, that he was unable to comfort me. So he had come there to exhort her, for God's sake, not to suffer that such a very young person might die from loving her so much, and that she should be blamed if she were the cause of my death. With his gentle and wise speech he warned my Lady to have sympathy for the malady in which, for her sake, I languished, for I was not at all recovering from the desire that was making me worse and that drove me toward wanting to see her. (2053)

When he had finished his explanation he saw that the exquisite, fair one was the color of death, and bore a very sad countenance, as he reported it to me. He saw clearly from her manner that my illness displeased her and softened her heart. Nevertheless she took another approach and said: "You are telling stories, fair Sir, saying that your cousin and mine is in such a state! By the apostle St. Paul, I hardly believe at all that he might conceive of such a thing. God, who would think it? But if that is so, surely Childishness and his very great inexperience in loving are impelling his heart; it could not be anything else. He'll be distracted from it in no time, if God helps you. Pull him out of it, if you can. Counsel and advise him to withdraw from this and to place his heart elsewhere. For he could never come near me, and great trouble could result were he seen doing so. I don't know how that old spy found out—God curse him! Because of him I haven't enough courage to speak to any mortal man. And if he were here now, I wouldn't dare speak to you. How could he tell that this child was inclined to love me? That man, filled with self-conceit, has worked my lord into a state, for he aroused Jealousy against me such that I wouldn't dare speak to anyone in secret. Wherever I may be, I must have a constant companion always at my heels, for he has been delegated as my guard. I have noticed that all this is due only to fear of your cousin. So he listens to what people say and relate to me, and he often goes to the door to observe who comes in here. By God, were it not for my conscience, I promise and pledge to you that I would have had him so badly beaten by my kinsmen, back and belly, that he would never again dare to install himself to watch me! To do so he would have to be a great fool. And so that this surveillance, which makes me so miserable, would cease, I sent to your cousin and urged that he hold back for a while and not come here, so that the spy might not see him. When the spying has ceased, he could come to see us straightaway. It seems to me that it is declining little by little, and I believe that without doubt Jealousy no longer thinks about it. Your cousin will be able to come here shortly, but I truly think it better that he refrain and not come now, if he's thinking about my welfare. As everyone testifies, love not seen is forgotten." (2135)

She responded that way to put me off, and gave me not even one soothing word, except in an ambiguous way. But my cousin did not accept that, saying instead: "There is such compassion in you, my Lady, that, whatever you say, I don't believe you'd let someone who is completely yours lose his body and soul; that's as true as the Paternoster, I say. And did you state that I can dissuade him from it? Indeed, if I take the soul from his body! I know no other way. Truly, I have made every effort to discourage him, but I tell you literally that he will die without help. You will have gained nothing if his days are shortened through losing

86

you. Virtuous Lady, tell me your answer, for I haven't an ounce of respect for the jealous one or his spies. They won't be such impressive guards that I can't fool them! Let me but see and perceive that you have some tenderness for him; offer him friendship, and be so very mindful of him that you want him to come here with me, and I'll fix him up in fine and fitting form. I'll handle matters so well that no one will recognize him. You have only to tell me what you want him to do and how he ought to conduct himself in order to see you. Now don't delay any longer, for he is quite eager." (2175)

She said: "Don't think that I am so much his enemy that his ill and discomfort do not displease me enormously. You understand, in truth, that I love him with a loyal heart. Let him take as his duty the protection of my honor, and without further delay I will do what should satisfy him. I don't want to say anymore at present, but let him behave prudently and not come here yet. Rather, you will come often, and will not converse with me in front of the watchmen. Send me your news through a certain careful person; he will come to meet you. This messenger is loyal, I assure you, but may neither you nor he confide in another, for that would displease me; nor would another dare to approach me. Now, you and I have spoken enough, and we don't know whether we're being watched. Let your friend be joyous and happy; convey to him that message, and tell him you have so persuaded me that as long as he makes no untoward request, he won't fail in his suit. And thus you will commend me to him and give him comfort, saying that before a week has gone by he will be able to see much of me. Let us take no further counsel now, but you will not leave just yet. We have been fortunate that Danger did not appear, so that we have conversed at leisure for a long while. You will please await my lord, who has not for some time had as much joy, indeed I know, as he will have when he learns that you are here. In the meantime, we shall play a game of chess. We can pass the time amusing ourselves that way." (2222)

Then without further discussion they began directly to play

on a sideboard. The master and lord of the place entered at the head of the room, and my cousin went to greet him. When the lord met him, he welcomed him handsomely and said that he was very happy about his visit and that he should feel welcome. In brief, without keeping you on this point longer, the lord honored him greatly and said that everything he had was at his command, and that if he thought to sojourn in the area he should come there and not take any other lodging but his. He would be completely happy to have him stay there, and would be quite displeased should he not. My cousin thanked him heartily. (2242)

The next day, after a light meal, he begged his leave and departed. He dashed back, for he knew that I wanted him to, and that I would soon be most joyous.

When he returned, he told me everything that had happened during his trip. He maintained that my affairs would go very well, for he would make frequent short visits there. By that means he would have both great and lesser people completely on his string, as he had promised my Lady, since he had her approval. He told and recounted everything to me, and my heart, which had been tormented by grief, became joyous. To get matters under way sooner, he advised me to write a letter in which I described my case completely and explained how Love was abusing me excessively because of her, and request that she hear the argument made by her servant, who was asking for her love—he sought nothing more! He advised me to put all these things in a sealed letter for which he would be the messenger, in order to soothe my pain. I put my confidence in him, so I dictated a letter in which I told how I was because of her love, and everything that was bothering me. I attached two ballades to the letter, which I sealed. Listen to this copy of it, you who are inclined to love. (2285)

Sealed letter in prose

To her who surpasses all others, whom my heart fears and adores:

Lady, flower of all sovereign ladies, highly revered and

praised princess, desire of my heart and pleasure of my eyes; with, first, my very humble respects; my greatly beloved and desired Lady, please listen with compassion and receive the plaint of your servant, who, as one under duress, like a man near death who takes desperate measures either to end his life or to live once more, very gentle Lady, to you who by your refusal have the power to kill me, and who, by the sweet comfort of your acquiescence, can restore me to life, I have come to ask for speedy death or imminent healing. Very beautiful Lady, I know that there is so much wisdom in you that you have been able to perceive how, for some time now, Love has held me and holds me in his nets because of you, and how Love, and the fear and fright that great love put in my heart, took from me the boldness to tell you so, sweet Lady. And I know very well, from every grace that is in you, that if you had known about all the pain and torment I have suffered since and suffer still, desiring your sweet love, the gentle compassion of your kind heart could not have left me in such lassitude—even though I haven't yet accomplished very many valorous deeds and there isn't in me sufficient valor to have deserved the love of even a far less important lady than you are. Ah, Lady, and if you protect your worth and high renown against my not yet having acquired the name of valiant, in view of my youth, you will have killed me! But, my revered Lady, consider that you can enrich me by giving me the courage and boldness to undertake and achieve, according to my powers, all the honorable things that the heart of a lover dares to think and do for the love of a lady. Sweet Lady and my goddess on Earth, since you can very easily raise up to high rank the man who loves and adores you as his most desired joy, please consider how, by your sweet comfort, he might be reprieved from death and given back life. And if you ask or want to know what has brought him to this point, I tell you that your very gentle, pleasing, comely, laughing and loving eyes have done this. Ah, Lady! since they delivered the mortal blow, it seems right to me that the blow must be softened and the wound healed by the sweetness of your pity. May it please you, very agreeable and honored Lady, to let me know your will and what path you wish me to take, toward death or toward healing. Nor do I wish to tire you with a long letter, but rest assured that I couldn't tell you everything nor write you exactly how it is with me, and understand that as a fact, whether I attain your love or not. For if I fail at it, you will see my death; but if, by grace, I attain your love, my good intention will show itself in serving you. Thus I send you the two ballades enclosed here; may it please you to receive them willingly, very beautiful and good Lady, whom I could not praise enough. I pray to God that He grant you as many good things and joys as I have shed tears for your love. Written with an ardent and desiring heart, your very humble, obedient servant. . . .

Ballade

Fair Lady, best and loveliest of all,
Have mercy on me, you who all decree
That I serve you. Body, soul I've let fall,
Per your wishes, and now my humble plea:
     You'll soon take leave
And out of pity, my pain you'll relieve,
Or for you I die, please do comprehend;
And so deign to accept me as your friend.

Alas, sweet flower, to whom I give all;
Don't kill me! I cry to you for mercy,
Praying, by God, since I'm engulfed overall
By pain, you'd cure me; I ask pleadingly,
     To seek reprieve

I know not where. I'll perish if you leave,
And see how I love without devious end;
And so deign to accept me as your friend.

Don't you see how you bid my tears to fall,
And that, if you help me too tardily,
I'm lost? For which, more speeches to forestall,
Kindly love me, for Love rules over me;
        Quickly, retrieve—
Deliver me, for my death I perceive,
You know I say this, the truth to commend;
And so deign to accept me as your friend.

My Lady, thanks! I do all you intend,
And so deign to accept me as your friend.

Another Ballade
(in diagonal wordplay)

Please have pity on me, my Lady dear!
Dearer to me, most beloved of all.
All free of pride, by me let your good cheer
Cherished be—priceless—fair blond, when I call.
Calm my flood of tears that o'er my eyes weighs
Ways to gain solace, which will my course stay.

If I fail because I don't prevail here,
Hear, strike me, Death: wounded I'd fall,
Fallow of heart, I'll no more persevere.
Everywhere I search, all misfortunes call
Callously to all. Love won't just give away
Ways to gain solace, which will my course stay.

Lovely one, to whom all virtues pay dear,
Earnest are you in faith, without equal;

Allow me as your serf—be not severe—
Verily, not cruelly, lest I in pain crawl.
Awl that pierces my heart, let me assay
Ways to gain solace, which will my course stay.

Lady, please send, as help to come my way,
Ways to gain solace, which will my course stay.

Just as you have heard, I wrote to my Lady and let her know
in writing of my miseries in order to gain her solace. My cousin
carried the letter. In no time he was before her door and indeed
had chosen the right hour to speak to her without Danger. He
then announced to her that my letter had come, about which she
in no wise grumbled, but rather received it laughing. Two or
three times, smiling, she read the letter and the ballades. Then
the beautiful, gracious Lady said: "I will write back to your cousin;
for the moment I'll tell you no more. And I'm going off to do
it before my chance to do so passes. You may entertain yourself
at chess and checkmate this Lady, my cousin." (2353)

Then she and her secretary, who knew how to keep a secret,
and no more than one other confidante (not another soul was
there), withdrew to a chamber. She began to put her thoughts
into words and dictated the letter as is here recorded.

Response by the Lady to the above-mentioned letter.

To my gracious friend:
  My fair and gracious knight, please know that I have
received your sweet, loving letter and ballades, in which
you acquaint me with your state of mind, in which you say
that if you don't obtain help quickly, your life must end. So
I write you my letter in order to respond to that. Understand that if you suffer so much because of me, all my heart
is heavy, for I would not want to be the cause of grief to
anyone. It saddens me more in your case than in another

because I know you. As for giving you comfort, which you ask of me, my dear friend, I don't know the intent of your request. But to tell you what I have in view: know truly that, should you ask me, or should I perceive, that you might intend something that could turn to dishonor, or to evil reproach, that is a goal you would never achieve. I would send you away categorically, of that you may be sure, for I would rather die than diminish my honor for any living soul. If it were the case, though, that the love of a Lady honorably given and without low thoughts might satisfy you, know that I am she whom Love has led to this, who wants to love you from this very moment on. I'm revealing to you so much of what I am thinking as to say that when I feel sure your desire can be satisfied by what I am willing to grant, I will want to have you for my only friend, beloved, on condition that your loving resolve and good intentions continue. If matters are as you have mentioned in your letter, that I might be the cause of your exaltation in valor, I am she who would ask of God no greater grace. Please write me your clear will on these matters. And yet, guard against allowing any desire to make you a liar in any way about something that might, in time, turn out to belie your words, for I would banish you completely from me. So I want you to chase away all melancholy and sadness and be happy, gay, and joyful. But above all I charge and enjoin you to be discreet. With what power is mine, I forbid you to have the custom common to many of your age: that is, not knowing how to hide anything and boasting that they have had more favor from their ladies than they've had. Take care, therefore, that you don't reveal yourself to friend or companion, however intimate, except when your need for assistance makes it necessary to reveal the identity of your dearly beloved. If you conduct matters thus and continue to do so, be sure that Love will not fail at all to bestow his wealth generously on you. My dear and fair friend, I pray God to give you all you might wish, for I insist that would only be all that is good.

> Written in joyful thought,
> Your beloved

When that letter was completed, my Lady got up and returned to my cousin. She gave it to him and told him that I should no longer be mournful, and he should tell me so; that she would strive to cure my malady; that she would fix a day, season, and hour when, before much longer, I would without fail be able to speak to her, and that she would name the place; that he should give me the letter and say she commended herself to me and ordered me to worry no longer. (2376)

My cousin thanked her and left. Upon his return he related to me what sweetness and goodness he had found in my Lady. And I, who was waiting for him in the fire and flame of great desire, raised my hands in joy, saying: "God, I thank you for having had mercy on me." He presented the letter to me, and I, who cherished this present, took it quickly and in great joy. When I had it in my hands, I believe I kissed it a hundred times! I read it not once but more than twenty times, I assure you, because I could not get enough of the comforting news I was hearing, which led me to rejoice and forswear my grieving and to be joyful instead, since that is what my Lady commanded and ordered. Thus was my hopefulness fully regained and no longer did I fear rejection, as I had before. Rather, I said I wanted to reply to her letter, and so I took paper, pen, pounce, and ink, and withdrew. Then in joy and untroubled, I wrote in the way I tell you here. (2411)

To the flower among the most beautiful ladies, my most revered mistress:

Very beautiful and good Lady, more so than I could say, whom I love, revere, and desire with all my heart; for whose sake Love, through the appeal of your beautiful eyes, made me become your true subject of my own free will, and in whose gentle service I am pleased and wish to spend my entire life, without regret, as much as I am able but not as much as I should. I thank you for your very sweet and pleasing letter which, through the comfort of sweet Hope, has brought back vigor and strength to my poor desolate heart, nearly perished from the despair of ever achieving your love. My very desired and honored Lady, to answer some points that you raise in your letter, namely, that you do not know the intent of my request, but, as to your own intention, you wish me to know that you would not diminish your honor on pain of death: I assure and reassure you, very sweet mistress, that my will is nothing but exclusively and entirely yours. For if I wanted anything but to do your will, I would not hold you as mistress of my heart and myself your subject. As to your saying I should guard against being the sort of person prompted by great desire to promise something that might later prove me a liar, my very beautiful Lady, I promise you surely and swear loyally, on my faith, that all my life you will find me as I am now; if not, I want and pledge myself to be banished from every joy and disgraced. As for concealing my secrets and guarding against telling them to friend or companion, except for what is beyond my power to conceal, sweet Lady, be assured that I indeed take heed—not in this or any other case in my power will you find fault. I thank you for the good counsel that you give me, sweet Lady; since I have given you assurance for all the circumstances that could have presented obstacles to me, may it please you to bring about what you have promised me in your letter: that, by your grace, you take me as your only loving friend; and if you find me disobedient in anything, let me be banished from your sight through my great disgrace. May God not allow me to live so long that now or at any other time I have the will to be false or deceptive toward you. As for the rest of what you say, namely, that you feel joy at being the cause of my advancement, sweet Lady, know that I will never attain it unless it is through you, for you alone can make or undo me. Sweet Lady, may it please you to comfort me and give me perfect joy by granting me your sweet love, and willingly satisfy my heart and my starved eyes by giving them the opportunity to see your deeply desired, sweet presence. In this matter please send me the very joyous news of what I desire. Sweet and charming one, esteemed above all others, I commend myself to you more times than I could say. I pray God that He grant you life and the will to love me truly. Written joyfully, in the hope of better fortune,

Your humble slave

Thus I finished my letter and at the end I inserted a ballade that was short so that reading it would not prove tiring. Listen to how it is, for it is in a strange guise: (2417)

Ballade

Nice and comely,
Where does repose
My heart, and she
In whom enclosed
Are all, held close,
Kindness and grace:
Pray, grant me grace.

Freshly, newly,
More than the rose,
Whose strife truly
I did disclose;
Piety chose;
A bygone case;

Pray, grant me grace.

Turtledove, see!
You, sweet and close,
Appeal solely
To what I glose.
Dare I propose
Love to your face?
Pray, grant me grace.

Lest you'd oppose—
Your heart forclose—
What I embrace,
Pray, grant me grace.

Through my cousin I sent back my letter, thus sending on his
way him whom I loved, asking him to implore my Lady to let
me speak to her soon and without delay, or I would shortly have
to end my poor, miserable life. He rode without stopping until
he arrived at her house. There no one gave him any difficulty,
rather he was well received. He behaved cautiously until he saw
the right time to report on the reason for his trip. (2458)

Then, in order to obtain some comfort for me, he spoke well
and wisely. He asked her, for God's sake, not to let me languish
any longer (I was dying so of love), lest an illness strike me from
which I might not regain my good health. He gave her the letter,
and she had the opportunity to read it all. In brief, her response
showed she believed I was speaking sincerely in my appeal for
her love, and, furthermore, that deception is not ordinarily placed
in such a young heart. She thought that was true, and she said
that without doubt, "Jealousy will leave within three days and
will go very far away—Danger, it seems to me, will go with
him. Then we will be able to converse together at our leisure."
As for choosing the time, she wanted me to accompany my cousin
in the evening, without making any noise, appareled as if I were

his valet. She further wanted someone to hide me when I arrived there so that neither friend nor stranger might know, except for her secretary. She would arrange the whole affair through that same person—how it would be done, and the way in which she wanted me to present myself there; my cousin had to tell me without fail that I should behave so nobly toward her that never would I do anything that incurred her displeasure or reproach. He reassured her, saying she could be certain of it, for I would dare do nothing but what she wished; I would rather die. So he came away with that news, so good and fine to me that in my great joy I thought I was dreaming. I thought about it every waking minute; still, the waiting seemed long to me. (2508)

On the day promised, she who had bound my heart to her did not forget to send for me. Thus I was glad to see the arrival of the very distinguished messenger who brought me the news I was longing for: I would go to the chapel, toward her to whom my heart inclined, who through this messenger was communicating what she wanted me to do and ordering me to tell no one except him who knew about it. My cousin and I and the secretary would go there, and would bring no other. We set out then and courteously took leave of our retinue. We told them not to be concerned about it and to be of good cheer, for the three of us needed to tend to a matter which would keep us all the day long, and that we would return the next day. We rode happily, without stopping. Exactly at the appointed hour, we arrived where my Lady sometimes resides. We got off our horses in the dark. Then I took off my clothes and put on others. My cousin, the good and wise man, went up without donning a disguise, and I watched the horses, being careful not to be recognized. When the time came, he invented the excuse that he had gone there at that hour for a pressing matter, something that had most assuredly just happened to him, about which, whatever the result, he must speak to the lord right away. Very great need made him hasten; this could not wait. He was told that the lord was not there, nor would he return for months. He replied that harm would necessarily ensue. Just then my very sweet Lady came running and appeared suddenly in an embrasure that looked out over the courtyard, and said: "What chance brings my cousin here? Lower the drawbridge quickly; thus I'll learn what he's asking about. I don't know whether someone isn't sending me pressing news through him." Then she sent two damsels to bring my cousin to her. When he came, she asked, after having greeted him, "Has someone been killed? Or what matter could bring you here so late? I haven't seen you for some time. Tell me what you are seeking." My cousin said that she shouldn't inquire further into the case. Since he had not found the lord and master, which troubled him, he would have to leave. She said that he must not do that, and that he must apprise her of his business without fail. "Then I must have my valet," he said, "who is keeping my horses at the gate, so that he may bring me a letter that I gave him for safekeeping; and he must be told to come without delay." Then, with unruffled demeanor, my Lady commended this matter to her secretary and he, providing very capable service, put the horses in a stable and led me upstairs. My cousin, who was being scrupulously careful, came to the door of the room and leaned toward me, saying: "Quickly! Give me the letter! Give me the letter!" To the secretary he said: "Let him be on his way in short order. He has no business here, nor is it seemly that a valet should remain in a chamber at this hour." My cousin spoke thus because there was a light shining in the room by which I might have been recognized, and that would have harmed me. He took out a long letter that I had placed in my bosom and took my Lady aside. In reading, he acted as if the letter described some important matter. In the meantime, the secretary, without any light, led me into the chamber of a lady who was prudent, discreet, and of blameless reputation, as my Lady had commanded she be, and who knew all about the matter. Her chamber adjoined that of my sweet, beautiful Lady. When the letter was read, my cousin, in plain sight of all, made as if to leave, and affected great sadness. But my Lady forbade him to go, saying that he must take lodging there or else she would complain to the lord, and thus she kept him there. (2631)

She did not converse at length with him but instead said it was time to go to bed, and she added that there was no reason for a man to watch over her in her chamber—no one need wonder about that. My cousin's lodging was prepared in a distant room, so there would be not a bit of suspicion or doubt about why he had come there at that hour. He was escorted to bed, accompanied by the most redoubtable men of her household; they were her guard, but she had no need of them at that moment. Then without delay, and in sight of her ladies, she disrobed and went to bed. But she did not remain there very long. Instead, she arose and dressed, inventing the explanation that she was feeling a bit poorly and wanted a fire made in the place where I was. So I was ushered out of sight until the serving woman had made a fire in the chamber. My Lady came dressed in a great cloak. No gathering of ladies came with her, just one. It was the lady mentioned before, whom she had chosen above all others, and my Lady came clinging to her. She sent the serving woman off to sleep, saying she did not want her to stand watch, lest she grieve about her Lady's illness. The door was closed after her. At that, the confidante came to get me and led me toward my Lady. I barely greeted her, for I felt such a stirring in me that I did not know where I was. Nevertheless I said: "Sweet Lady, God save you, both body and soul!" "Welcome, friend," she said. Then she bade me sit next to her, for as soon as I saw her I became a man enraptured. My Lady noticed this and received me with kisses, for which I humbly thanked her and expressed my gratitude. (2684)

The Lover

Then my revered Lady, my heart's feared and respected one, began thus to speak.

The Lady

"Have I done your will, fair Sir, I who have had you brought here secretly in this way? Is this the act of a loving friend? Do not deceive me; give me a complete accounting of your thoughts, if you can, and do so while you have the chance, I beg you earnestly."

The Lover

Completely dazzled with joy, sighing, I said: "Ah, sweet Lady, and what should I say? By my faith, I cannot speak! So take it in good part and note how I am yours entirely, body and soul, very dear Lady; more than that I could not tell you." And then she drew closer and put her arm around me. Laughing, the Lady spoke as follows.

The Lady

"So I must speak for the two of us, since you cannot think of anything to say? But then, I do believe that Love sends me such an overwhelming serving of his favors that I cannot voice what I thought you'd say nor what I'm to say—of that I could not utter a word."

Then the other lady who was there began to smile and said, without hiding anything: "What clever company! Do I see that you've come to this point already? I can see that Love makes even the wisest foolish, that I know well." (2724)

The Lover

My Lady says to me: "Friend . . ."

The Lady

"Since Love has thus put both our hearts in one prison, no longer is it necessary to ask whether you love me and whether I love you. I believe that Love claims us, or can proclaim us both, his servants, which does not grieve me. Nevertheless, sweet friend, since I place myself in your confidence I want to disclose to you all my desire, without concealing anything. I do not know what your intention is, but I say to you that whatever love you see in me—no matter what secret thing, sweetness, or pleasure in love, word, or appearance I give, and even though I may embrace you and kiss you—do not believe that ever, any day of my life, I have the will or desire to commit a base act that might leave me open to every kind of reproach. Sweet friend, thus I warn you, because I would not want you to say I have given myself to you halfway; for never will the day come that I feel so powerfully summoned as to do something that diminishes my honor. I swear to you truly that as soon as I perceive, by your appearance or countenance, that you have any other intention, you will never see me again, not even once, I assure you, even if you hate me for it. But as for all the other pleasures that a lover may take from a Lady, I wish to refuse you none and you may dispose of them at will. I give you my heart entirely, and abandon to you everything that I have, short of committing a folly or doing wrong. I promise you loyalty and faithful love, and I choose you above all others, if you can be satisfied with that, for I am telling you the truth. Tell me your will while you have the time and opportunity, for I want to hear what you have to say." (2780)

The Lover

When she whom I revere had explained all her thinking, I answered: "Ah, my Lady, my heart nearly faints away to hear you speak thus! Would this not satisfy me—the love, the favors, and the grace that you bestow on me? I trust you may never imagine I would not be completely in accord with whatever you wish. Now, believe me truly, just as I wrote to you in answer to your letter, that I accept, promise, and swear to you, under pain of perjury, never to be honored, but entirely dishonored, if ever a day in my life, in deed, in word, or in intention, I do or think anything in my power, either in secret or in public, which might displease you. Test me entirely as you may wish, for never will anything that your heart might want displease me, nor will it ever happen that I grieve to do your will. Must I thus be sad? Are you not my Lady? Is it not right that I conduct myself as you wish? And should I take a desire to do otherwise, may the life and soul be snatched from my body, and tormented! God! Does it not rightly suffice that I see you love me and call me sweet friend? Do I not have what I desired? I was seeking nothing else. I consider myself well rewarded if only you will always be willing to love me thus. I know that there is not a bit of falseness or lack of pity in your heart. And yet I am of the opinion that I will do so much by way of service to you that I will be even more loved by you. So command me from now on, for I am your liegeman; my heart and body and soul I submit to you, beautiful Lady. Now command your pleasure, or send me where you please; I will go, and in everything I will obey your will, without contradiction. You can, as you desire, do with me more than I could say, and may God watch over you and exalt you for promising to love me completely. I must not inveigh against Love, who put me on the path toward attaining such noble joy. So I thank you humbly, beautiful and good Lady, for I will wear the lover's crown from now on. It will remove from me every ugly stain, and I will take on and pursue the task honorably in order to follow in the steps of the valorous. Thus you will make me a worthy man, sweet Lady. In sum, I could not be happier, so much that I can hardly say it." (2860)

Then my Lady, in whom all grace resides, embraced me very sweetly and kissed me more than one hundred times. I remained in that comfort all night, and believe, you lovers who hear this, that I was indeed comfortable! Many a sweet word filled with joy was uttered that night, and she in whom all goodness resides taught me how and where I could see her very often, no matter who might be displeased. Thus I went roving no more, for I had everything I wanted. She nevertheless charged me to guard her honor and so to delay coming to see her for some days, for I might put her at risk, even though staying away might be a torment. She told me I should instead await prudently the day and time to come, and she assigned me a day to return. We spent our time together like that, but the night passed quickly for me. When morning came, which troubled me, she said, "Adieu, my sweet love," embracing and kissing me one hundred thousand times and keeping a sweet and loving face. She locked me in there all by myself and went off to her own bed. (2894)

Afterward I was led out, in the costume of a page, by that wise man, the secretary who'd been informed about all this. And though I'd not learned anything about it, I took up my first office once more. Keeping the horses at the gate is good when one receives such a privileged appointment—the compensation is so sweet and agreeable! As for me, I would absolutely not want to be employed in any other capacity, and may this pleasing occupation be useful to me often! So you see how sometimes the master must master the valet's role—and perhaps that happens often to the man who gets his wish! (2912)

My cousin got up in the morning and made no noise, not wanting to wake anyone who might be sleeping. He had taken leave of my Lady the night before and so remained no longer. He came out; I was waiting for him and brought the horses forward like a good and well-behaved valet. He said: "Come here! the fever take you, boy, the way you lean on the saddle!" Thus he spoke in the presence of others, for knights and footmen wanted to accompany him home and were blaming him for not having more of his people with him. But he had done it expressly, for a specific reason, he assured them. He thought he would find the lord there, for he never had greater need in his life, nor greater desire to speak to him. And now he did not want anyone to accompany him, and he got underway. (2938)

Thus we left, and while riding spoke many a gentle and gracious word, because the sweet thought of returning there and of the delicious pleasure I had enjoyed was so comforting to me that no man might have greater joy at any price. We soon neared my residence, so much had we spurred the horses on, but I had donned my own attire once more. Then my people, who love and respect me, received us with great joy as soon as they saw us coming. We were joyous, too, and thus with happiness, in a spirit of pleasing renewal, we sang this brand new virelay: (2958)

Virelay

Beauty, where lie all my joys,
Your love makes my heart rejoice,
Of which with greatest glee
I sing, my pretty lady,
For whom love's fury I'd voice.

Yet to me you have now sent
Sweet succor, which has consoled
Me, and hastens my ascent
To joy, whose words made me bold.

For 'tis right that I by choice
Offer smiles, for gloom destroys
Solace; thus 'twas lost to me.
But softened is all ennui
Through your aid, awaited voice.
Beauty, where lie all my joys.

Since to me you did present
Your gentle heart, now behold
Me elated and content,
Restored to joy and consoled.

Ah, my Lady, Love's envoys
Bring sweet comforts when my choice
Resorts to Him. Pale I'll be
No more, since, allied with me

He adds hope for our re-voice,
Beauty, where lie all my joys.

I have recounted to you how I was first caught and tamed by
Love, and then how I was led on harshly by great Desire, and
how my dear kinsman worked so hard in order that my pain
might be ended through my Lady, who had mercy on me, thanks
be to her! Now I'll tell how things have gone for me since and
how they still are.

From that moment I was cheered, as you have heard, and in
my joy I recited this ballade: (2999)

Ballade

There's none more content than I, to Earth bound,
For to my joy no other can compare,
Since she whose peer or equal can't be found
Has granted me favor. Were I to bear
My love unto death, my suff'ring and care
Would sure reward have, most wonderfully,
From her for whom claims I humbly propound,
Since she has given her sweet love to me.

Ah, Beauty, in whom all values abound!
You wish no more that for you I despair,
So you'd have it that to all lovers 'round
I reply: "I am he who hungered where
Love gives out his bounty; empty, I frowned."
But then my dear, crowned with gen'rosity,
Saved me; my blaming Love was without ground,
Since she has given her sweet love to me.

Now did gales of play and laughter resound
From bitter tears I'd sown in despair,
Through which gay, chic, and with pure thoughts I bound

More than ever before. Love's shown me where
The path goes, and to me my Lady fair
Sends pleasure so much that joy's set me free
On all sides; and how toward all good I fare,
Since she has given her sweet love to me.

Prince of love, to complain I should not dare
About having pain, for joy was to me
Restored by her, who led my heart from care,
Since she has given her sweet love to me.

I kept myself elegant and well-dressed: clothes, horses—I
wanted to have more than a thousand beautiful things—and I
made a great effort to know everything appropriate to good people.
As I could, I avoided what was unseemly and always had in mind
increasing my renown so that my beloved Lady might consider
herself loved by a valorous man. Thus I exempted none of what
I had from being used in noble pursuits and, to all appearances,
I kept no account of my extravagances. To be brief in my story,
I tell you truly that I had no other aim except to follow the path
of true lovers and of the sweet, delicious favors that Love and
ladies give out to the loyal men who do not leave them. Heavens!
I often received her favors, for I took the road more or less every
week (though some difficulty was unavoidable) to the place where
I would see my sweet goddess in great happiness once more,
without a soul knowing it or anyone noticing it, except those in
whom we confided. The first time I went back to see her I brought
this new ballade to her, which pleased her greatly, and came away
with one in return. (3063)

Ballade

Command me to do, my Lady revered,
Your bidding—I'm poised to do as you say!
As with your serf by whom loved and most feared

You are, with me you can now have your way;
　　　In rightfulness.
I've held to this, for in you my joy rests,
More no lover has ever chanced to meet,
For your presents are more than others sweet.

Since you've caused all my suff'ring to be cleared,
And proffered all necessities my way,
Aren't you right to collect from an endeared
Heart—one wishing you pleasure to purvey?
　　　Ah! What mistress
To her servant grants reward so gen'rous
In Love's gifts? The rest to others I cede,
For your presents are more than others sweet.

Early on for me, budding Love appeared
Within my heart, when I received such pay
For serving well; ne'er from me to be steered
For as long as I live. Gentle one, stay,
　　　Comforteress
Of my vigor! My Lady, your highness,
Other gifts but this only grief entreat,
For your presents are more than others sweet.

　　　Gentle princess,
I enjoy much pleasure at your address,
No longer desire nor with languor meet,
For your presents are more than others sweet.

　I had a response to my ballade before I parted from that very
sweet creation, who gave me more than an ounce of very loving
joy, for that beautiful, exquisite one, in reading it, put her arms
about me, thus: (3099)

Ballade

Blessed be the very day,
The site, the place and repair—
Gentle friend—where, led this way,
I was. So long have I dwelled there
    That I conveyed
All my love. Friend, no better gift I may.
For this I praise Love, who did this contrive,
Since from it most perfect joy I derive.

Since I gave myself away
To him who no pain could spare
For me, now people will pay
Me honor; this did I dare
    Before midday,
Yet right I was to love him; if gainsay
His doubts I did to heal him, 'twas to thrive,
Since from it most perfect joy I derive.

So I came, like New Year's Day,
Friend, should God of me take care,
For the Fates in favor weigh
For me sweet solace to bear,
    For which repay
You I did early, for drowned in dismay
I'd long made you be. From this I revive,
Since from it most perfect joy I derive.

    When well away
In love with you, I gave my heart free play
In all delights, with no misdeed to shrive,
Since from it most perfect joy I derive.

That is how joy was granted to me, as you hear, and so I led
a joyful and amusing existence. But soon after, Fortune, who is

ready to destroy lovers when she can, thought to do me grave harm, as I'll tell you briefly now. It happened—it didn't take long—that the Lady who knew about our love and who shielded our activities had business in her lands, where she would have suffered damage to her inheritance had she not gone there quickly. She left the court downcast and pained, and for my own part I was greatly saddened. I knew that without her there was no means or way that I might see my Lady, which gave me great distress. For certainly, without seeing her, nothing could please me. My Lady knew it well—I believe that, for her part, she had hardly less grief. (3154)

Then she thought of another lady who had served her more or less all her life, who was wise and discreet, good and loyal, and could keep a secret, but who no longer lived at court. She wanted to try to engage her once more, if possible, so without delay she wrote this letter to the lady, and received her answer. (3165)

To my very good and dear friend, the Dame de la Tour:
The Duchess

Very good and dear friend, please know as to my condition that I am in health, thank God; may He grant the same to you. I write you because of the desire I have to see you and to talk to you. I haven't forgotten the good and fine service you have always done for me, for which I am so much obliged to you that I could not repay you. Rest assured that you have a friend in me, and that you may put it to the test whenever it pleases you. Dear mother and friend, you know very well how I am governed here and held in extreme submission and fear and treated roughly, and that my lot is very hard, which gives me little pleasure, and how I have not a soul to whom to complain and tell my secret thoughts. I would not reveal them to anyone but you, from whom I would conceal nothing as from my confessor, for I know you to be so reliable that I could confide in you. So you may know that it greatly distresses a young heart always to live in disagreeable circumstances and without any joy at all. Thus I would like you to be near me; I would tell you about some very charming things, which I am not putting into writing to you, for good reason. I need your help and advice, and so I beg you, in the name of all the love you have for me, that, once you have seen this letter, you put your affairs in order as quickly as you can, such that you are ready to come to me within a week from then; I will send for you with all due honor. Do not regret leaving your household in the slightest, for I promise, upon my faith, to reward your effort so hand-somely that it will always be to your advantage and to that of your kin. I beg you not to fail in this and to send me, with the bearer of this letter, your favorable answer. Send greetings to me, your adopted daughter. Good and dear friend, may the Holy Spirit hold you in His sacred keeping. Composed in my castle, January 8th.

My Lady sent a messenger on his way with that letter to the lady whom she called her very good friend and whom she loved dearly. Her friend sent a response that troubled me greatly, for it was very much against me, and it warned her thus: (3173)

My very revered Lady, first, I offer my deeply humble respects; may it please you to know that I have received your very kind and loving letter. I thank you with all my poor heart because you do me so much honor by remember-ing the meager service I did you in the past, which was not at all as sufficient as would suit your worthy and noble person, and by regarding me more highly than I could merit in all my life. My very dear Lady, as for coming to you now, please allow me to be excused, I beg you most humbly, for by my faith, my daughter is so gravely ill that I could not leave her under any circumstances. God knows how troubled I am that because of her malady, my revered

Lady, I cannot speak to you as soon as I might like. I am bound to counsel you for your good as someone who has been in my tutelage from childhood until now, however unworthy I may have been. It seems to me that I would err in remaining silent about what I know might bring you grief if I didn't point it out to you. For that reason, dear Lady, I write you what follows in this letter, about which I implore you most humbly not to bear me ill will in any way, for you may be sure that very great love, and the desire ever to increase your noble renown and honor, move me to do this.

My Lady, I have heard rumors about your conduct such that I am saddened from the bottom of my heart, for I fear the ruin of your good reputation. And the rumors are of the ruinous kind, as it seems to me: it is right and reasonable for every princess and high lady, as she is raised high in honor and status over others, to surpass all others in goodness, wisdom, manners, personal traits, and comportment, so that she may be the exemplar by which other ladies, and similarly all women, may govern themselves accordingly and as may be appropriate. Let her be pious toward God; and let her have an assured, quiet, and calm demeanor, and be moderate in her amusements and not noisy; may she laugh quietly and not without cause; may she have a noble manner, humble countenance, and stately bearing; may she respond kindly to everyone, and with an agreeable word; may her costume and ornaments be noble but not overdone; may she welcome foreigners in a dignified manner, speaking with restraint and not too familiarly; may she reflect thoughtfully upon matters and not be flighty; at no time should she appear harsh, cruel, or injurious, nor, in being served, too severe; may she be humane and kind and not too imperious toward her serving women and servants, and generous with gifts, within reason; let her know how to recognize those people who are the worthier for their goodness and uprightness, and the best among her servants, and let her draw them to her, men and women, and reward them according to their merits; let her neither believe nor trust flatterers, male or female, learning to recognize them instead and chasing them from her; let her not lightly believe things she is told; may she not be in the habit of taking counsel with stranger or friend in a secret or solitary place, especially not with any of her retainers or serving women, so that it may not be judged that one of them knows more of her private affairs than another; and let her never laugh and say in front of other people, to no matter what person, any veiled words not understood by all present, so that those within hearing may not suppose some foolish secret between her and that person; she must not keep herself in her chamber and too alone, nor must she be too much in sight, but let her at times withdraw and at other times appear in public. And though these qualities and all other manners suiting a high-ranking princess may have been yours in the past, you are at present completely changed, according to what people say. For you have become much livelier, more talkative, and gayer than you used to be, and commonly, that kind of conduct, when demeanor changes, makes other people judge that hearts have changed, too. Now you want to be alone and withdrawn from people, except for one or two of your women and some of your servants, with whom you hold counsel. And even in front of people, you laugh and utter innuendo, as if you all understood each other well, and as if only their company pleased you and the others could not serve you to your liking. Those things and the appearance they give are reason to move your other servants to envy and to cause others to judge that your heart has, somewhere, fallen in love.

Ah, my very sweet Lady! for God's sake, consider who you are and the high position to which God has elevated you, and do not consent to forgetting your soul and your honor for some foolish bit of pleasure. Do not place your confidence in those vain thoughts that many young women have who bring themselves to believe that there is no harm in loving in true love provided that it leads to no wrongful act (for I feel certain that you would not want to conceive of matters otherwise, on pain of death), and that one lives more happily because of it, and in doing this one makes a man become more valorous and renowned forevermore. Ah! my dear Lady, it is quite otherwise! For God's sake, do not deceive yourself on that score, and do not let yourself be deceived! Take a lesson from such great ladies as you've seen in your lifetime who, simply for having been suspected of such a love, without the truth of it ever having been ascertained or known, lost their honor and saw their lives ruined. There were such women; and I maintain, upon my soul, that they never sinned or acted in a basely culpable way; and you have seen their children reproached for it and less esteemed. Although for every woman, whether poor or rich, such foolish love is dishonorable, it is much more inappropriate and injurious in a princess and in a high-ranking lady, the more so as she is important. The reason for that is a good one, for the name of a princess is carried by everyone, and so, if there is any stain on her reputation, it is known throughout foreign countries, more than in the case of ordinary women. The reasoning is right, too, considering the children of princesses, who must rule lands and be princes of others, and so it is a great misfortune when there is any suspicion that they may not be the legitimate heirs, and many difficulties can come from that. For let us suppose that the body commits no misdeed: there are those who simply hear it said that such and such a lady is in love and they will not believe at all that there has been no wrongful act. And because of but a bit of unguarded foolishness, committed by chance out of youthfulness and without misstep, evil tongues will judge and will add things that never were thought or said. Thus such talk goes from mouth to mouth, never diminishing, always increasing. So it is necessary for each great lady to be more careful in all her habits, demeanor, and words than other women. The reason is that when one comes into the presence of a great lady, each person looks at her and listens to hear what she will say, and attentively notes everything about her. Thus the lady cannot open an eye, utter a word, laugh, or give any appearance that will not be received, noted, and retained by many people and then reported in many a place. Do you not think, my dear Lady, that it might create a very bad appearance for a great lady—indeed, for any woman—when she becomes livelier and gayer than is her wont, and seeks to hear more talk of love, and then, because of something that happens, her heart changes and she suddenly becomes sullen, ungracious and quarrelsome, and no one can serve her in a manner that pleases her, and she does not care about her clothing or dress? People surely then say that she was in love and no longer is. My Lady, that is hardly the manner a lady ought to adopt, for she must take care, whatever her thoughts may be, that always her bearing and appearance prevent such judgments from being made about her. But it could well be difficult to maintain such composure when one is leading a life of love. For that reason, the surest way is to avoid that life and flee from it completely. So you can see, dear Lady, that every great princess—and, similarly, every woman—must be more eager to acquire a good reputation than any other treasure, for it makes her shine with honor and it remains forever with her and her children. Revered Lady, as I mentioned earlier, I can well imagine and envisage the reasons propelling a young lady to incline herself toward such a love: youth, ease of situation, and leisure make her think, "You are young, pleasure is all you need. You can well love without baseness. There is no evil in it when there is no sin. You will make a man valorous. No one will be the wiser. You will live more happily because of it and will have acquired a true servant and loyal friend." And so on. Ah! my Lady, for God's sake, take care that such foolish ideas do not deceive you! Because, as for pleasure, rest assured that in love there is a hundred thousand times more grief, searing pain, and perilous risk, especially on the ladies' side, than there is pleasure. For along with the fact that Love by itself delivers many different kinds of bitter moments, the fear of losing honor, and that it may all be known, remains in women's hearts continually and makes them pay dearly for such pleasure. And as for saying, "This will not be evil, since it will not be a sinful deed," alas! my Lady, no one, no woman, may be so sure of herself that she becomes certain, whatever firm resolve she may have, always to maintain moderation in such a love and that it will not be known. As I said above, that is certainly an impossibility, for there is no fire without smoke but there is often smoke without fire. And as for saying, "I will make a man valorous," indeed, I say that it is a very great folly to destroy oneself in order to enhance another, even if we suppose that he may thereby become valorous! She indeed destroys herself who, to refashion someone else, dishonors herself! And as for saying "I will have acquired a true friend and servant," Heavens! and how could such a friend be helpful to the lady? For if she had some troubling matter, he would not dare step in to help her under any cir-cumstance for fear of her dishonor. Therefore, how can such a servant serve her who will not dare to apply himself for her good? Now, there are some who say that they serve their ladies whenever they do any number of things, be it with arms or in other ways. But I say that they serve themselves, since the honor and the profit remain with them and not at all with the lady! Still further, my Lady, if you or another wish to excuse yourselves in saying, "I have an inconstant husband who gives me little pleasure and loyalty, and for that reason I can, without committing a misdeed, take pleasure in another in order to forget my melancholy and pass the time"—surely, such an excuse, saving your grace and that of all other ladies who utter it, is worth nothing. For he who sets fire to his own house in order to burn his neighbor's commits too great a folly. But if she who has such a husband bears with him patiently and without damaging her reputation, so much the more will the merit of her soul, and her honor, increase in praiseworthiness. And as for pleasure, certainly a great lady—indeed, any woman, if she will—can, without such a love, find many permissible and correct pleasures to which she can give herself and pass the time without melancholy. For those who have children, what more gracious pleasure can one ask, nor more delight, than to see them often and take care that they are well-nourished and well-taught, as pertains to their high rank or station, and to see their daughters trained from childhood to acquire the rule of living properly and as befits them through the example of the right company. Alas! and if the mother did not conduct herself in an entirely prudent manner, what example would that be to the daughters? And for those who have no children, it is certainly honorable for every high-ranking lady, after she has said her prayers, to employ herself in doing some handiwork in order to avoid idleness, or to have fine linen made, marvelously worked, or silken sheets or other things that she can make use of; such occupations are worthwhile and prevent a person from thinking idle thoughts. I do not say that a noble young lady cannot amuse herself, laugh, and play in seemly fashion at the right time and place, even where there may be lords and gentlemen, nor that she must not honor foreign visitors as befits her high station, each according to his rank. But this must be done so soberly and with such fine deportment that there is not a single glance, nor a laugh, not a word that is not carefully weighed and governed by reason. And always, she must be on her guard that no one may perceive in her words, glance, or countenance anything unseemly or inappropriate.

Ah, Heavens! if every great lady—every woman, truly—really knew how attractive to her this fine bearing is, she would take greater pains to have it than any other finery, for there is no other precious jewel that can adorn her as much.

And further, my very dear Lady, it remains to talk of the perils and risks that are in such a love, which are without number. The first and greatest is that one angers God, after which, if the husband notices it, or the kinfolk, the woman is ruined or fallen into reproach, and never after has any respectability. Yet let us suppose that does not happen; let us talk in favor of lovers: although all may be loyal, discreet, and truthful (which they scarcely are: instead, it is well enough known that commonly they are deceitful, and in order to trick women they say what they do not intend or want to do)—it is nevertheless true that the ardor of such an affair does not last very long, even for the most loyal, and that is certain. Ah! dear Lady, when it happens that this love has subsided, can you conceive of how the lady who has been blinded by her envelopment in foolish pleasure bitterly repents when she realizes what she has done and reflects upon the follies and various perilous situations in which many a time she found herself? Can you conceive of how much she might wish it had never happened, no matter what the cost might have been, and that such a reproach could not be said of her? You certainly could not imagine the enormous feeling of repentance and the distasteful thoughts that remain in her heart. In addition to that, you and all ladies can see what folly it is to put one's self and one's honor at the mercy of tongues and in the hands of such servants—since they call themselves servants, but the result of their service is commonly such that, whatever they may have promised you and sworn to keep secret, they do not keep quiet at all. At the end of such love, moreover, people's blame and their talk remains with the ladies; at the very least, there is a fear and heartsick dread remaining that the very ones in whom they have placed their confidence may tell of it and boast, as might someone else who knows about it. Thus the ladies put themselves freely in bondage, and there you see the result of that love service! Can you conceive of what a great honor it seems to ladies' "servants" to be able to say and boast that they are loved, or have been, by a great lady or lady of renown? How then would they keep quiet about the truth? For God knows how they lie, and God be willing that, among you, ladies, you learn that well, for you would have cause to protect yourselves from it. Because I know that you like ballades and poems, my Lady, I send you one, composed on that subject by a good master, if you would please note it well. Now, as for the servants who know your secrets and in whom you must trust—do you believe, by your faith, that they keep quiet about it, however much you may have made them swear to do so? Indeed, the greatest part of them are the sort who would be very sad were it not known that they have a greater familiarity and boldness with you than the others; and if their mouths do not actually tell your secrets, they hint at them in various covert ways that they want others to notice. Ah! Heavens, what servitude for a lady and for every other woman in such a situation who will not dare to reprimand or blame her serving man or woman, in the event she sees them commit a great error, since she feels herself in their power. They will rise up against her so arrogantly that she will not dare say a word, rather having to suffer them to do and say

things that she would not tolerate from any other. And
what do you think those servingmen and -women say, who
see this and note it? What they are thinking is only what
really is, and be sure that they whisper about it a good deal.
And should it happen that the lady becomes angry or
dismisses her servants, God knows that everything is
revealed and talked about in many places. Moreover, it
often happens that servants are and have been the means
and promoters through which this love is plotted, and it is
something they have pursued willingly and assiduously in
order to gain gifts, offices, or other emoluments. Very
revered Lady, what can I say to you? You may be sure that
one would as soon drain a great, yawning chasm than
recount all the perilous evils that are in this life of love.
Nor should you entertain the thought that it might be
otherwise, because that is how it is. For that reason, very
dear Lady, do not place yourself irretrievably in such peril.
If you have given it some thought, for Heaven's sake,
withdraw before a greater evil befalls you, for it is much
better sooner than later, and later better than never. You
can already see what words would be said if you continued
your new ways, since they have already been noticed, and
word of them is broadcast in many a place. I do not know
what more to write you, except to beg you humbly, with
all that is in my power, to bear me no ill will for this, but
rather let it please you to take note of the good will that
makes me say it. And besides, I should want to do my duty
in loyally warning you, even should I incur your displeasure, than to counsel your destruction or keep quiet about
it in order to remain in your favor. My Lady, please note my
ballade, which I send you enclosed with this letter. Very
revered Princess and my dear Lady, I pray God that He give
you a good and long life, and Paradise. Written at La Tour,
the 18th day of January.

> Your humble creature
> Sebile de Monthault, Dame de la Tour

Ballade

Women of honor, preserve your renown!
For Heaven's sake, the contrary eschew
Of honor, may none upon you frown;
Trouble not to make acquaintances new
Such that they'd record and bring to view
That in your bearing loose morals be found,
Or that in some case you'd deign to misdo;
And stay away from the false gossip hound.

For seeming well-loved, like a worthless crown,
By many folk, yields such small revenue
As dishonor by random gossip sown
In different places, once in you they view
Easy virtue. Thus for you must ensue
The public record, unless you say nay
To the evil often with folly wound,
And stay away from the false gossip hound.

Now with perfect sense arm yourselves down
Against those who seek so much to undo
Your good names, and whose slander you have known
To be without cause, but who, to please you,
Feign courtesy. For this my retort's due,
When I often hear those whom you're around
Speak ill of you—please keep above their hue,
And stay away from the false gossip hound.

Women of honor, please don't misconstrue!
If I advise you on how to confound
Deceivers, trust me, no more words I'll spew,
And stay away from the vile gossip hound.

Thus the Dame de la Tour, who put me in very difficult circumstances by the letter she wrote back, sent that response to

my Lady, who was deeply troubled by it. But she did not hate her as a result, rather she said: "Alas! would that it had pleased Our Lord that the Dame de la Tour might have remained with me: she would have counseled me to do the right thing, and I would not have been lulled by bad advice. But, in the end, I will cease this and follow her counsel, for I can see clearly the harsh peril to one's life that comes from a life of love. But he of whom I am thinking very much must also withdraw from this." Then she wrote such a letter to me as you will now hear: (3221)

Sealed Letter

My fair friend, it is indeed true that Foolish Love, who deceives many, and the unguarded pity that I had for your laments, have led me to forget what I should keep in mind unceasingly: my soul and my honor. I have indeed proven that I have already put myself in many great dangers and risks to satisfy your youthful desires and mine—although, thank Heavens! there has been no baseness, nor will there be; may God not let me live so long! Nevertheless the world would not believe as much if some misfortune befell me from it. I can see that whoever throws himself into such foolish love is hardly master of himself or of his comportment; and so, such love will necessarily be noticed, as you can see from the long letter that the good and virtuous Lady, the Dame de la Tour, wrote to me, which I in turn send to you so that you may understand the reason impelling me to withdraw. For when I gave myself to this love, I took no notice of the perils into which I was flinging myself. But this wise Lady has opened my eyes to reason and to considering my situation; and if I failed to do that, I would be ruined and dishonored. And, dear friend, you should not at all want that; that is why I beg you please to withdraw. Know that I make this request of you in spite of my feelings and with my eyes filled with tears, for no one could be loved more than I love you. So do not think this comes from a lack of love, for I swear to you on my portion in Paradise, and promise you on all the oaths that can be made, that as long as I live, you will be my only love, and I will always love you, excluding any others, even if love doesn't remain in you; nor do I dismiss you from my love, for you have not deserved that from me; nor could my heart, which loves you, consent to it. Rather, you must only cease coming to see me, for the harm that could come to me, which I know would be a sad and grievous thing for you. But while your heart will be sick over it, mine will hardly be in good health. I do not know what more to write you, nor am I able, for my languishing heart, my eyes, and my face, are all filled with tears, and I bid you farewell, my fair love.

Your sorrowing Lady

When I had read this painful letter, I lost both pulse and healthy color, and I was as if dead. I did not revive for some time, for I had fainted from the misery I felt at hearing the news that I had to flee, banish myself, and withdraw from my Lady. Never had I experienced such disagreeable fortune; I wept so much from it that I almost plucked out my heart. I read the long letter that had caused this thing, and God knows, as I read it, if I didn't curse the old woman who had sent it! I would gladly have drowned her, would that act have eradicated this situation! When I had endured this sinister sorrow for a long while, without any abating, I wrote the following letter, wetting the handwriting with my tears. (3245)

To the most sovereign among ladies:
    Alas, my sweet and revered Lady, my sovereign love whom I serve, fear, obey, and adore: where could I find the words sufficient to declare to you and to make you understand thoroughly my great sorrow? For tears and weeping

cloud my thinking and my memory so that I do not know where I am nor what I am doing. Alas, my Lady! Now you have brought me low by your harsh letter saying that I must withdraw from you. Certainly, it is the truth, whatever that Dame de la Tour may say about lovers, that I am yours more than anything else you may have in this world, and that I have promised to obey you completely—a goal I will keep all my life—without transgressing against anything you wish, to the best of my ability, as indeed I give you to understand. But when it comes to abandoning my love for you, that I cannot obey, for I have given myself for life, so it would not be in my power, even on pain of death, to stop loving you. But, dear Lady, to obey your commandment that I no longer see you, if it pleases you that it be so for all purposes, then I will have to resist seeing you with all my strength. If you command me, though, not to die, not to lose my mind, I will not be able to obey, I know it truly. And so that you see that I desire your honor more than does she who has written you about it at such length, I will go to die in Outremer in order to remove all suspicion that you might be the cause of my death; nor will I ever return from there, I swear it to you by my faith, and thus you will find it to be. Alas! and in what place, just to plot my death, did she find that there are already rumors and gossip about our love? Truly, she invented it! Saving her reverence, it cannot be, for never was anything so cleverly and so secretly conducted up to this very moment as our sweet love has been, and always will be, if it please God. For God knows that I would sooner suffer death than do anything that might dishonor you. Ah, my Lady! Ah, my Lady! then will I never see you again? Since it will have to be so, may God grant that I lose my sight and no longer see a thing, for nothing else could please me. And how then would my heart endure or remain alive, since it would no longer have the joy it receives when near yours? Alas, miserable me! Alas, this thought is a lance that pierces my sorrowing heart—as does the realization that I must thus lose, without good reason, the sweet comfort, the loving pleasures, the pleasing glances, and the delightful words that I received from you, whose sweet memory and souvenir, alive in my thoughts in the hope of returning to them, kept me joyful and happy more than any other man could be. My very sweet Lady, since I must die without having deserved it, a single gift I ask of you, for the sake of all the love your sweet, noble heart once had for me, and do not behave so cruelly to your poor servant as to refuse him: it is that before I am dismissed entirely I might speak with you once in order to take my leave and bid farewell to all the sweet things you gave me lovingly, when never, upon my soul, did I have a base thought or one not in accordance with your will. Alas, my Lady, I know well that you do wrong to all those sweet things and make them suffer harm without cause, for I maintain firmly that this dismissal is not what they agree to or wish. Dear Lady, may this gift be granted to me! I do not know what more to say to you, but be sure that I will obey you until death. May it please you to tell me soon which of the roads you wish me to take, whether the road to Outremer, as I have said, or whatever road pleases you. And please pardon me if this letter is stained with my tears for, upon my soul, it was not in my power to restrain them or to make them cease until I had written the letter. Revered Lady, I commend myself to you more than I could say, and I pray to God that He give you all the good things that are to be wished for. Written in deep discouragement, in tears and in weeping.

Your poor love, the unhappiest of men

I sent that letter to my Lady, and wept mightily in offering it. I remained crushed, grieving and trembling; and, lamenting, I uttered this ballade, while venting my sad plaints: (3251)

Ballade

Ah, Death, Death, Death, I bid you come to me!
Carry me quickly from this world of pain,
I no more wish to live, since my lovely
Wishes me to retreat afar. To wane
Make my poor heart, with grief and suff'ring cursed,
Since I myself from joy and sadness cleave,
I choose with none but you, Death, to converse,
Because my Lady has asked me to leave.

Alas, alas, what a grievous story!
Ne'er did blows from lance, sling, or dart sustain
Any man before, who heard so cruelly
Such news as I have, so thus to unchain
My distress—more than I can say in verse—
Since distance myself from love's heights this eve
I must, I go mourned to a death most terse,
Because my Lady has asked me to leave.

Ah, Lady, would you treat me so harshly
That you'd suffer me such grief to sustain,
For your love? I call for testimony
From Love, who knows that in this age's reign,
You'd find no truer in this universe:
No better man to deed and word achieve,
But all my efforts go from bad to worse,
Because my Lady has asked me to leave.

Ah, God of Love! Why, Lord, aren't you averse
To my death—unjust, sad—without reprieve?
For I lose all; for me there'd be no nurse,
Because my Lady has asked me to leave.

Just as I describe it to you I replied to my Lady. When she
had opened my letter and when she saw it so covered with tears,

the writing erased and defaced, she surely became desolate, as was reported to me, and, while reading it, wept so much that tears streamed down her face. Then, taking mercy, she wrote back to me in great haste. She charged the messenger to carry her letter quickly, and he took it upon himself not to stop until he had brought it to me. Bearing the urgent letter, the messenger did not stop all night long until he finished his journey at break of day before the castle gate. Then he brought me the letter that comforted my grief and took away my tears and misery. I needed that sorely, for I was certainly on the way to losing my life or my mind. Listen to what the letter said that she sent, at which my heart was joyous. (3309)

To the fairest and best of all, my true and loyal love:
    My true, loyal, very sweet and fair love, the truth is that as I was frightened to lose my honor (which I must care about above everything, having been advised in this matter by the Dame de la Tour's letter, as you have seen, to whom I am grateful, since I know she counseled me for my own good), I wrote you what I did in my recent letter despite my feelings. But, my gentle and gracious love, I see that Love could not suffer our separation, and I repent greatly of having sent that message. I know you have had and still have great pain because of it, for which I beg you to forgive me. I ask your forbearance, and it grieves me that our good friend, your cousin, is not with you to comfort you, and it displeases me that he has gone on such a long voyage. I beg of you, with all the authority I may have with you, and on the love you have for me, that you please return your heart to its deep peace, as it was before. I fear you may have grown so sad that I will not come in time to comfort you, and that some malady—God protect you from it!—may take you; and because of that, I will not rest easy until I hear news of you. So I write in great haste, beseeching you to be glad and of happy demeanor, for I can tell you good

news: our dear friend, in whom we confide, will be here in four days. You will come to see me, and I will send for you, and we will rejoice as before; for God help me, were I to die for it, I could not let you go! And I hope that, with God's help, our affair will be hidden and that you will always safeguard my honor, for I have confidence in that. My sweet and fair love, I pray to God that He give you perfect joy. Written hastily,

Your true and loyal love

After I had received that letter I conquered my misery. I wept no longer, adoring God instead for that very good news. I wrote my answer and thanked my Lady profusely. I also asked to see her soon so that I might tell her about the pain I had suffered on account of her earlier letter. (3321)

There is no point in my making this account longer. It is time that I stopped—you have heard everything, how I enjoyed the love I wanted, without baseness. For, to the person who may say so, I deny that in our love there was any ugly or base deed, or that loyalty was ever breached in any way. For that reason, our love ought to be the more praised. And on the other hand, I have also told you about the torments and lamentations that were mine, and how I accumulated so many that my Lady took pity on me. Now it is time to bring this tale to an end, for if I were to recount all the adventures, some pleasant, others harsh, that happened to me in the course of that love, both the good and the bad that came to me from it, I might be tiresome, for I would have much to say and the telling would be without end. But to finish briefly, I tell you that after that letter, I saw the lovely one on whom I depended many a time in many an amorous encounter. From her, whom my heart will not leave, I received a large measure of Love's gifts, charmingly given. And that lasted fully two years, without lying, and she would not let me leave the country. That pleased me just as well as it did her, for so ardent was I that I took account of nothing but being near her. Thus I believe I visited her more often than I should have, so that smoke went up from what we were doing, kindled by evil tongues. I was sad, destroyed, for I could not put out the fire. I could no longer see my Lady as I used to, which weighed heavily upon me. I was blamed by my friends and called a coward for remaining too much inside the country, where I frequented only jousts, tourneys, and revels that were held in the vicinity, never venturing far. That was not very seemly for a gentleman, to tell the truth. They said I would be the worst of my lineage if I remained there longer and did not take up arms in many a land to acquire praise and valor. (3383)

That was the sermon my kinfolk intoned to me. They importuned me so much that I heeded what they said for my own good, but I feared my Lady would be displeased if I did what they said without properly begging my leave of her, and I was sick at heart. I asked her to arrange that I might speak to her, for I had to go abroad for a while, especially for her honor, and I asked her to believe firmly that I would never forget her for even a day. I would go to Spain, where men were going—it was better to do that than let worse happen. Thus I reminded her of my promise that for her love I would do so much that, in sum, I would acquire a reputation as a valorous man. I worked and plotted so much that, with difficulty, I managed to speak to her, for our meeting was short and she came at great peril wherever I was. There were tears, great sorrow, and long faces at our parting, and reluctantly she consented to my going off to war. As we embraced tightly and in deep despondency, wetting each other's neck and face with tears, I commended her to God's keeping, and I commended myself to her one thousand times, submitting myself to her will. I promised her that everywhere I went I would write her with my tidings, and she would write back and tell me how things were with her. Thus I departed, weeping and in sorry condition at leaving my dearly beloved. I joined an army in Spain and was there for a year, far from my fair one. Then I wended my way back, desiring to see her. (3433)

When she heard news of my return, she arranged for me to speak to her without it being known. I was received with joy. We were happy together, and we talked of how we had missed one another. Thus from time to time I went there, but I spoke to her at her peril; she came secretly, fearful and trembling, frightened of being watched, and greatly afflicted. When I saw her so troubled, a great part of my joy was dissipated because of the danger in which I saw that she placed her honor and herself for my sake. For that reason I undertook many a voyage. I sailed to Outremer, because of the danger of gossipmongers. (3454)

Thus for ten years I led that life, during which I often came and went. Upon my return it sometimes happened, when it was seemly, that I would see my dear Lady. In that way I traveled through many a land. I became a prisoner of war after a hard battle, and my Lady was distressed. Thus I suffered hardships aplenty before the ten years had passed. Love himself dealt me many of them and did not release me; for although I never, on my soul, saw anything in my Lady that might cause me to doubt her that I could tell, Jealousy, which is madness, mixed such a brew for me that I became like a madman. One time I returned from abroad and as soon as I looked at her I thought her feelings toward me had changed, and it seemed to me she had completely abandoned me; such chagrin overwhelmed my heart that I went mad. Thus I lost all joy and could not calm myself for a long time nor appease my heart, which despaired. My Lady was so displeased with me I almost lost her favor. (3491)

Then too, if I dare say, I once saw her a little jealous, which troubled me deeply, for I knew no reason, nothing to explain why that had come about. God knows that I never deceived her either in thought or in deed, nor did I cast my eyes elsewhere to contemplate another lady. But I understand that whoever has the flame of love secure in her heart must slip into a jealous state, for someone who bears in her heart a great and perfect love can hardly renounce jealousy. (3506)

And so we wrote many a lyric about our affair: now of grief, now of surcease. I recited ballades that I composed about our various states: lais, complaintes, other poems, of which there was one happy one for every ten sad ones—that's the way of a foolish heart that Love leads astray. My Lady sent me some in return, whenever she could appropriately do so. You will shortly hear, after this, what thoughts we expressed in our poems, which soothed our pain when we were far from each other. This is how we diverted ourselves in the hope of better, however long that might take. (3525)

I have recounted the beginning, middle, and end alike of the love from which, for ten full years, I suffered hardships and troubling thoughts. Nor has that same love passed away, nor will it disappear before we die. But scandalmongers, whom God should destroy, for there are too many of them in the world, have forced me to abandon my visits to her to whom I have promised my love without regret, and she will not see me lie. But I saw her receive dishonor because of me, since everyone was whispering about the situation, for which I came to despise my long life. For that reason, to guard her honor and her peace, I preferred to delay seeing her, although I proclaimed myself unfortunate and sad many a day, since she had been brought to such blame on my account. But nevertheless, my body and wealth, and whatever I have to give, is hers. If I had to I would die for her, and that's no lie. So I pray to God Almighty that He grant her peace, honor, a good and full life, and never-ending joy. And here I end my tale. (3559)

Here ends the book called The Duke of True Lovers

> To all poets of learning
> Who are bent upon learning
> Whoever composed this tale,
> 4   Since ev'ry verse did entail
> A free or leonine rhyme,
> They're in this work all the time.

Now this fruit of my labors
8   Must be judged by my neighbors
Without me, as rhyming verse,
Whether good or the reverse,
May a vowel before not sound
12   Nor last syllables resound,
Save for in rhyme perfected.
Thus she tried to perfect it,
To show her intelligence;
16   For knowledge and diligence
Are required to versify,
To conjoin and diversify
Many subjects various:
20   Some nice, some nefarious.
If you doubt what's here as proof,
Go and test your own reproof,
Record your own sad affair
24   If this strikes you as unfair.

Ballades in Several Ways

I

Fair one, I must take my leave
And my distance from your gaze,
At which I must sorely grieve;
4   I'll die of chagrin in days
Since my spirit, which no longer plays
Upon perceiving your sweet mien,
Which is, as my judgment says,
8   The most perfect I've e'er seen.

—My love, consent I'll not give
To your departure, nor grace;
Without you, my heart will heave

12 In torment: penance's brace.
 And I'm pained when my thoughts trace
 How usurped from me he's been:
 Him whose excellence conveys
16 The most perfect I've e'er seen.

 —Lady, I must, I believe,
 Sell all my goods, since love pays
 Enough for two; each receives
20 Rightful shares—so none blame lays
 On me. Since I can't phrase
 My defense, my rage is keen
 For you, heart of wisdom's grace,
24 The most perfect I've e'er seen.

 —Where'er you might spend your days,
 My love, faith I pledge to mean
 That you are—here no doubt weighs—
28 The most perfect I've e'er seen.

II

Ballade in Responses

 To take my leave, sweet mistress,
 I've come: farewell, 'til we meet again.
 —Alas! My love, this brings me dire distress,
4 For your leaving will cause my death by pain.
 —Fair one, myself to you I commend
 And pray God all your due rewards to send.
 —My love, my grief has not ceased,
8 But do not forget me, at least.

 Alas! What shall I do when my "comfortess"
 I no longer have, for you kept me sane.
 —My love, help me, for in woman weakness
12 Lies where there's none in men; by this I'm slain.

—Sweet flower, I see it to rend
My heart with grief, and that toward death I tend.
—My love, do quiet your pleas,
16   But do not forget me, at least.

I leave my heart with you, sweet mistress,
For God's sake, seek no other to name.
—Never think, my love, that a traitoress
20   I'd ever be; for you are all my gain.
—Lady, without still delaying the end,
To my departure I should now attend.
—My dear, whom I love so, go in peace,
24   But do not forget me, at least.

—Good-bye, fair one, may God defend
You from woe, and highest recompense send.
—Good-bye, I weep unappeased,
28   But do not forget me, at least.

III
Ballade in Double Rhymes

Lady, I go from you pallid and wan,
Won over by grief, from which I sigh,
A sight worse than I was ne'er come upon:
4   Pungent Death's taint has turned my life awry;
I now must despise my life's lengthy rule,
For truly my death would not be so cruel.

Oh, vile gossips! With the Devil begone!
8   You've gone to harm many, so may God decry!
Cry out I must, for all good lies in one
Woman who grieves; because of you, I,
With ire filled, cannot endure its accrual,
12   For truly my death would not be so cruel.

•

Indeed, fair one, your sad plaints caused to run,
And won, more tears than mine, though my pain's nigh.
By inches I'll weaken; my appeal done,
16   Only you will pity me: my pained reply,
Highest Lord, spare me this arduous duel,
For truly my death would not be so cruel.

I'd sooner die, no more life's renewal,
20   For truly my death would not be so cruel.

IV

What can I do if I moan
        And bemoan
My most dolorous loss,
4   Blatant cross
Upon me: the gift I possessed,
        Then distressed
Me, with grief my heart is sown.
8   Thus I groan,
For I gave my mortal dross;
        No gain was
Mine; so I pine, tears expressed,
12   My love's best.

When the sweet friend called my own,
        Makes well known
His valor, this none will cross
16   With good cause,
That is clear (my joy's bequest);
        Ne'er more jest
Can my heart, whose health once shone;
20   It's now prone
To torment. At a loss—
        Stricken pause—
In grief, I alone addressed

But in vain strife overblown
     My heart's thrown;
No path I e'er come across
28   Toward me draws,
That I some glimpse of him wrest,
     From which, lest
My heart too loudly intone—
32   Falsely done,
No—but from a heart shorn of flaws;
     One sure law's
For him in whom I attest
36   My love's best.

There's no cover I might toss,
     Nor fine gloss,
For to hide my interest:
40   My love's best.

V

Sad and suff'ring, at death's door,
     Peace no more,
My sweet Lady, love's domain,
4   I'm far, on a distant shore,
     Sicklied o'er;
With my face of grave pallor,
     I remain.

8   From you I hear nothing more
     To succor
Me with joy; I thus sustain
The fear that you might ignore
12   The accord
Between us; thus in rancor
     I remain.

•

Indeed, if you never more
16   As before
Thought of me, you'd cause me pain;
Grief would put me at the door—
      Fate most sore—
20 In you, truest paramour
      I remain.

My Lady and sweet domain,
Where my heart has ceased to soar,
24   'Tis the core
Of my worth; without succor
      I remain.

VI

If you forget me one day,
Sweet love, I'll no more be gay,
      I'll no more bother;
4 For I suspect that you may
Have given your heart away
      To love another.

For some time, I've been dismayed
8 As no letters come my way,
      And I shudder
For fear you did convey
Your feelings without delay
12   To love another.

Thus my love you would betray
Mortally; under your sway
      Do I smother
16 In your love, if sworn to stay
You're not—this time, gone astray
      To love another.

I, pale as whey,
20   You've not deserted me, pray—
That your love you'd not purvey
To love another.

VII

Lady, toward a humble end
I myself to you commend
And thus seek to let you know
4   How things have stood.
Know that strong desires contend
To see you, should time portend
Such news as you can bestow,
8   All well and good.

Sound in body, at wit's end,
My mind's torment's loath to mend
As mem'ries I won't forgo:
12   Wild pangs withstood,
Recurring as my thoughts defend
All your graces without end,
Which are there, the truth to know,
16   All well and good.

And while my journeys extend
So far, only grief's a friend,
As duty summons, I go
20   Though some folk would—
Be they women, be they men—
Prevent me; so with care I'll wend
My way to your charming glow,
24   All well and good.

My God intrude,
And grant all that you intend

Without limit, as here penned
28   August first, where none are, know,
        All well and good.

                    VIII

        Sweetest love, my anguish you have consoled
        Since I've received good tidings from you:
                In point you're well,
4   Thanks be to God, and I've also heard tell
        That I'm not forgotten, which thrills me anew,
        No better news to me could e'er be told.

        From where my life stands, my comfort extolled,
8   At present I'm well, but I've suffered too.
                The cruelest spell
        Has often pricked me, but now you dispel
        My heart's suff'ring, with joy it's riven through;
12   No better news to me could e'er be told.

        And with this have you my joy foretold
        By your return, whence I'll share bliss with you.
                May God grant well
16   That I see you, and our hearts as one dwell,
        For then I'll enjoy a blessing most true
        No better news to me could e'er be told.

        May this reach my ears without much ado;
20   No better news to me could e'er be told.

                    IX

        Gentle Lady, no more can I endure
        So far from you. And so must I return
                Most presently
4   To your side, or my demise I'll assure;
        It grieves me to be far, this long sojourn,

Most certainly.

I'm impatient to see you, 'tis sure,
8   Lovely one, for there's nary a soothing turn
         To what pains me
But you, naught more; none other can cure.
My sweet, noble, courtly one: hear and learn
12   Most certainly.

Now I come back—no longer to abjure,
To God the Teutonic tongue I return,
         And equally
16   Germanic ways—for you, serene and pure,
I must back to French countryside adjourn,
         Most certainly.

         Most joyously
20   To see you, fair one, my route I secure
For France, and leave the land of beer-filled urns,
         Most certainly.

Virelais

I
Welcome back from travels past
More than I know how to tell,
Friend, I've no more to compel
4   Since you've returned at long last.

Indeed, I have waited so long
So that I'd see you again
My heart's own desires burn strong
8   For you, but no other men.

Alas, did your mem'ry cast
Only me and thus dispel
Other ladies? I can't tell;
12   I know not if that has passed;
Welcome back from travels past.

My tired heart lost its gay song;
But now that it's seen again
16   Your lithe form, with which I'd long
Been kept well, my heart will tend

Toward sweet solace, there held fast
With you, where no ire will swell;
20   Since I have you, just as well;
I know not where grief has passed.
Welcome back from travels past!

II

Good Lord, my Lady most sweet!
If we can blamelessly meet,
        To see you
4   I pray: your calm pureness anew
        Cutting neat;
Be quick, or upon my soul,
        I'll die true.

8   For I've come intending this,
Trav'ling from a distant land,
And if I should fail, sweet miss,
I shall believe that I stand

12   Hated by you. For beneath
A tomb love's fiery heat
        I'll push, to
Ease my heart. Oh, may you view

16   Me effete

With desire, whose flames defeat
        All I do.
Good Lord, my Lady most sweet!

20   So please don't be too remiss
(Or I'll be a troubled man)
In see'ng me—for I'll not miss
This deep pain I now withstand.

24   Perhaps 'tis to all discreet,
I'm not sure. I'd ne'er mistreat
        Dearest you;
I'd sooner death suffer through;
28   I entreat
Your aid. Oh! My heart's faint beat
        Prays for you.
Good Lord, my Lady most sweet!

III

My love, for me nothing's right
        Lest you might
Come back to me. Grave pain
4   I suffer now; with my might
        I hold tight
To harsh mem'ries of my plight
        And deep pain.

8   I dare not look up again
        Nor would fain
Traverse the threshold aright;
Strangely on guard I remain
12   Where I gain
Suff'ring, which I must by right

Keep treasured and recondite
    Or indict
16 Myself should my honor stain,
Which I've for life kept in sight
    To do right
'Til blue in the face; I've tried
20   As you name.
My love, for me nothing's right.

Thus the awakening bane
    Who's germane
24 To Danger, whose curse would blight
All my goods, with pride so vain,
    Cause me pain
And my misfortune incite.

28 Thus must I finish by right,
    Bring to light,
For lachrymose I remain
Desiring to hold you tight,
32   Joy invite
Via Fair Welcome to reign
    Here again.
My love, for me nothing's right.

Rondeaux

I

Now must I begin to mourn
For failure at my intent
To see my Lady content,
4 By other cares I'm not borne.

•

My desire and will conformed
To no other incident;
Now must I begin to mourn.

8   My resolve I'll not reform;
For all sorts of pain I'm meant.
Since she from me is absent,
No prize is equivalent;
12   Now must I begin to mourn
For failure at my intent.

II

If I've in error returned
    And now turned
Your graceful form to discern
4   Before meeting your sweet eye,
    I'll not lie;
Lady, of remorse I'll die.

My being will shift astern,
8   Overturned
In languor, and yet all churned,
If I've in error returned.

Only sadness I'll have learned
12   If I'm spurned;
No more your fair gaze I've earned.

In hopes that others comply
    I'll rely—
16   No, of this grievous ill I'll die
If I've in error returned
    And now turned.

III

Alas, I cannot retell
　　　My ire's hell.
Fair one, I must go away
4　　　To foray
Out of this torture cell,
　　　Angry well.

Not seeing you, I might as well
8　　　Ne'er dispel,
The helplessness felt each day
Alas, I cannot retell.

Nor can I discern so well
12　　　How befell
My least of ills, though I sway
　　　And give way
To heartbeats doctors can't quell
16　　　Where I dwell.
Alas, I cannot retell
　　　My ire's hell.

IV

Lovely one, for whom all pain I endure,
With mordant regret from you I depart:
Departure that makes my heart come apart.

4　For I must leave you, sweet portraiture,
Lovely one, for whom all pain I endure.

And as I take leave, dark mis'ry is sure;
Because you assent to breaking my heart,
Ceaseless torment is my lot from the start,
8　Lovely one, for whom all pain I endure,
With mordant regret from you I depart.

Complaint

More than all others ailing,
To you, Love, I'm bewailing
The pain within me railing
4   And the torment
Of the path you've me scaling
From which my hope's cruel failing,
My tortured heart assailing,
8   But by ire rent.
I know no medicament
For you, my predicament,
From bad to worse each day's spent,
12   My soul flailing.
And at all that I attempt,
I fail, then sigh and lament.
At this price, I must resent
16   Life's retailing.

For I was by you deceived—
Now this knowledge I've conceived—
Though tardily, I've perceived.
20   Well I should die
When I summoned and received
Him by whom I feel upheaved
In sorrow, and who achieved
24   Remorse in my
Purpose, which made my heart sigh,
He, his face pale as if to die,
Told me he was smitten by—
28   So he's perceived—
Me above the rest; that I
Was his love, with words he'd ply
Me so that, moved, I'd comply,
32   Having believed.

And so much did he complain,
Sigh and moan, his pallor plain,
That, thinking he couldn't feign,
36   My heart I'd say
Caused him such plaints to unchain.
Thinking the best I'd attain,
My trust I didn't restrain,
40   And went Love's way.
This happened to me in May,
But in joy I found dismay,
For I shut myself away
44   With Danger: no greater reign
O'er me was. My heart I lay
Enclosed with him whom I'd say
Was my sweetheart; and that way
48   I gave free rein.

At first, my heart thus taken
Went on, sweetly mistaken;
For turning pale and shaken
52   It seemed he stood
Before me: so my stake in
Love doubled, to awaken
Greater with such signs taken.
56   For die he would
Lest help quickly to him should
Come; he seemed more stiff than wood,
And water streamed in a flood,
60   Doubly breaking
O'er his face, so that he could
Not speak; such grief he withstood,
As if lying on thorns for good,
64   For dead taken.

All these signs saw in him there

I did, and more, say I'll dare,
My heart ravaged in despair:
68   Love's loss and load.
Thus I had, enough to spare,
A friend of form and face so fair,
His charm sated everywhere.
72   In this abode
I lived long within this code,
And still do, but my blood slowed
For pain's clamor to erode,
76   I here declare.
Just then did my fear forbode
Losing him, my bad name sowed.
As one who once with love glowed,
80   I to you swear.

Since he whom I had consoled
Himself once nicely controlled
Toward me, such faith did uphold,
84   That to amend
I knew not, and, made so bold
By Love's words, he thus took hold
Of me, so that I'd behold
88   Joy, and could send
For him and also command,
As with my serf; without delay,
My peace he wished to have stay,
92   And thus consoled
My heart was indeed—the way
He looked at me, truth be told—
No better wish could demand
96   One mortal-souled.

Alas! But how he has changed
At present and how estranged

From me, by which all enraged
100   My heart now feels.
For well I see how they've gauged
Him against me, since he's changed
His mind; he's now engaged—
104   A new love seals
His heart; this the deed reveals,
He no more pleads nor appeals,
No longer the path he steals,
108   This I've presaged,
And, as a good lady steels
Her worth, I hear his appeals,
Open what my heart conceals,
112   So he's encaged.

Thus I'm his mortal conquest;
It began with his strong request
So much that I could not rest
116   Where'er I'd be,
Then elsewhere he took his quest,
No more he loves me the best.
Yet with his love I'm obsessed
120   Where'er I flee,
For in him quite shamelessly
I've placed my love, all of me.
And now I must rightfully
124   Assume the pose
Of grieving pain, joylessly,
Since by such a path I see
I lose the one dear to me,
128   Truth to disclose.

And if to leave me he chose,
Of his welcome I'd dispose
As I should—his disdain shows—

132   He separates
Himself from me, whom he knows
For my honor, virtue—those
Virtues prized, how he'd depose
136   Me, the fact states;
Yet elsewhere his heart relates,
I see well; mine palpitates
With pain while it contemplates,
140   As my mind knows,
That we're no more, which creates
Grief in my heart, which equates
With death, which dissociates
144   Us in harsh rows.

Nothing's gained by my complaint
Nor my face tear-stained and faint,
For he'll ne'er, except in feint,
148   Love me the same.
Since another he's attained,
And my love cast off, disdained.
So I'll stay in sad constraint
152   And he will claim
Another love as his aim,
Their engagement he'll proclaim,
From which my poor heart will rain
156   Tears unrestrained!
But never will it disclaim,
Fore'er to affirm the same,
Until death shall me reclaim,
160   Which leaves me pained.

Glossary

Page numbers in brackets refer to the first or unique appearance of an item.

Allemande. The Allemande or Almayn, which originated among the Germans, was a stately dance later lightened by the introduction of hops between the steps. It may have been quite new in Christine's day. [60]

arrow of love. See Sweet Look. [53]

barre, **casting the** *barre.* A game or sport played by tossing a stake or tree trunk; like casting weights. [50]

blunted tips. The point of the jousting lance was fitted with a coronal, or crown-shaped tip. The blunted, or rebated, end reduced the chance of fatal injury. [62]

bodice. The French word is *corsés.* Its precise meaning is not known. Worn by both sexes in England and France throughout the fourteenth century, it sometimes may have been an open mantle or gown. Sleeves seem to have been a later development. The poet and chronicler Froissart says in his *Espinette amoureuse* that a *bel corset* is worn to dance (l. 3216, see Newton, pp. 15, 25, 32–33), which indicates the garment's elegance and suitability for festive wear. [63]

commençaille, or *commençailles.* The tournament was generally introduced by *commençailles* in which individual knights fought before their companies entered the events. In this, the tournament and warfare itself were similar, since a joust between two champions was a frequent prelude to battle. (See Juliet R.V. Barker, *The Tournament in England 1100–1400,* pp. 40–41, 141, 152. [64]

Danger. A courtly allegorical commonplace, Danger often represents all that is opposed to love, that stands as an obstacle. In *The Romance of the Rose,* Danger is a guard at one of the doors of Jealousy's tower, in which the Rose is imprisoned (see **Jealousy,** below). [39]

device(s). A heraldic motto or emblem affixed to the arms and often making a punning allusion to a name. [64]

high saddles. Used in tournaments, the high saddle raised the rider up nearly to a half-standing position and offered support under the legs and sometimes behind the back. [64]

high table. The high table, or table of honor, was on a slightly raised platform. For a festive occasion the dining tables would have been set up in a rectangle, and the order of seating went according to the diner's rank, as the text here shows. [61]

Jealousy; jealous husband. Personified Jealousy is another common courtly figure (see **Danger,** above). In Guillaume de Lorris's *Romance of the Rose,* Jealousy builds a prison tower for Rose, the young man's love object. Related to Jealousy is *Le Jaloux,* the proprietary older jealous husband of much courtly literature who stands in the way of his (younger) wife's amorous pursuits (and pursuers). Interestingly, in *The Book of the Duke of True Lovers,* it is rather the spy who is described as a *viellart,* or old man, probably because it would be unseemly for the princess to denigrate her husband. [86, 87]

jewel. It was customary at French and Burgundian tournaments to offer a jewel as prize. (See Barber and Barker, *Tournaments: Jousts, Chivalry and Pageants in the Middle Ages,* p. 191.) [59]

old woman. The Duke's reference to the Dame de la Tour as an old woman recalls the Duenna or Old Woman (sometimes translated as Old Lady) in *The Romance of the Rose,* a portrait to which Christine de Pizan took exception (see Introduction). [79]

Outremer. Originally the collective name given to the four crusading states of Antioch, Edessa, Jerusalem, and Tripoli established in the Holy Land by the European leaders after the first crusade. It later came to refer to any place "beyond the sea," as it seems to mean here, although it still has overtones of the crusade as a means of forgetting one's love. [130]

painted lances. The pageantry of tournaments was enhanced by the many colors borne by both horse and rider. In the case of lances, it was usual to paint their shafts. (See also, Introduction.) [64]

Round Table. A frequent enhancement at tournaments, Round Tables could include enactments of stories from Arthurian literature (see the *Dictionary of the Middle Ages,* Vol. 5, p. 350), although the Duke's does not. Sometimes they were a political means to an end: at a Round Table in 1344, for example, Edward III of England invited foreign knights, whom he hoped to win to his cause (see Juliet R. V. Barker, 67–68). The Duke's Round Table seems to be intended simply as a means of inviting everyone, including the "foreign knights," to dine together, and thus to create good feeling among all. [68]

selion. Normally refers to a measure: the area of the strip of land between two parallel furrows of an open field. Here it seems to refer to the strip of land itself. [64]

Sweet Look. In many medieval romances love is said to begin as an arrow that enters through the eye, thus at the sight of the beloved, who must be beautiful or handsome enough to inspire it. The arrow then travels to the heart, where it lodges. In Guillaume de Lorris's *Romance of the Rose,* one of Cupid's arrows is named Sweet Look. [53]

sweets. Often taken for refreshment or before retiring, these could be spices, fruits, and nuts (licorice, coriander, juniper berries, dates, anise, almonds, hazelnuts, dried raisins, apricots, oranges, lemons, ginger) preserved with honey: a comfit. [60]

venans. Those who were the defenders were called the *tenans* and those who challenged them, the knights "from outside," were the *venans.* (Christine uses only the term *venans.*) [59]

Selective Bibliography

1. REFERENCE WORKS

Kennedy, Angus J. *Christine de Pizan: A Bibliographical Guide* (London, 1984).

Yenal, Edith. *Christine de Pizan: A Bibliography of Writings of Her and About Her* (Metuchen, New Jersey, and London, 1982). Second edition: *Christine de Pizan: A Bibliography.* Scarecrow Author Bibliographies, 63 (1989).

2. TRANSLATIONS OF CHRISTINE DE PIZAN'S WORKS INTO ENGLISH OR MODERN FRENCH

The Boke of the Cyte of Ladyes, tr. Brian Anslay (London, 1521). Reprinted in *Distaves and Dames; Renaissance Treatises for and about Women.* Ed. Diane Bornstein (Delmar, NY, 1978).

The Book of the City of Ladies, tr. Earl Jeffrey Richards (New York, 1982).

The Book of the Duke of True Lovers, Now first translated from the Middle French of Christine de Pisan, tr. Alice Kemp-Welch, with Laurence Binyon and Eric R.D. Maclagan (London, 1908; rpt. New York, 1966).

The Book of Fayttes of Arms and of Chyvalrye: Translated and Printed by William Caxton from the French Original by Christine de Pisan, ed. A.T.P. Byles (London, 1932, rev. 1937).

The Book of the Three Virtues. See *A Medieval Woman's Mirror of Honor; The Treasure of the City of Ladies.*

The Fayttes of Arms and of Chyvalrie. Facsimile of Caxton's 1489 edition (Amsterdam, New York, 1968).

Le Ditié de Jehanne d'Arc, eds. and trs. Angus J. Kennedy and Kenneth Varty (Oxford, 1977).

The Epistle of Othea to Hector, tr. Anthony Babington, ed. James D. Gordon (Philadelphia, 1942).

The "Epistle of Othea." Translated from the French Text of Christine de Pisan by Stephen Scrope, ed. Curt F. Bühler (London, 1970).

Christine de Pizan's Letter of Othea to Hector, tr. Jane Chance (Cambridge, Mass., 1990).

The Epistle of the Prison of Human Life, tr. Josette Wisman (New York, 1985).

Le Livre de la Cité des Dames, trs. Thérèse Moreau, Eric Hicks (Paris, 1986).

A Medieval Woman's Mirror of Honor: The Treasury of the City of Ladies, ed. Madeleine

155

Cosman, tr. Charity Cannon Willard (New York, 1989).

The Middle English Translation of Christine de Pisan's Livre du Corps de Policie, ed. Diane Bornstein (Heidelberg, 1977).

Morale Proverbes of Chrystine. Facsimile of Caxton's 1478 edition of Anthony Woodville's translation. (Amsterdam, New York, 1970).

L'Oroyson Nostre Dame: Prayer to Our Lady by Christine de Pisan, trs. Jean Misrahi, Margaret Marks (New York, 1953).

Poems of Cupid, God of Love: Christine de Pizan's "Epistre au dieu d'Amours" and "Dit de la Rose"; Thomas Hoccleve's "The Letter of Cupid"; with George Sewell's "The Proclamation of Cupid," eds. and trs. Thelma S. Fenster, Mary Carpenter Erler (Leiden, 1990).

The Treasure of the City of Ladies, tr. Sara Lawson (London, 1985).

La Querelle de la Rose: Letters and Documents, trs. Joseph L. Baird and John R. Kane (Chapel Hill, 1978).

3. RECENT MODERN EDITIONS

Lavision-Christine. Introduction and Text, ed. Sister Mary Louise Towner (Washington, D.C., 1932). (A new edition is in preparation by Christine Reno.)

Cent Ballades d'amant et de dame, ed. Jacqueline Cerquiglini (Paris, 1982).

Christine de Pisan's Ballades, Rondeaux, and Virelais : An Anthology, ed. Kenneth Varty (Leicester, 1965).

Christine de Pizan, Le Livre des Trois Vertus, ed. Charity Cannon Willard, with Eric Hicks (Paris, 1989).

Christine de Pizan's "Epistre a la Reine," ed. Angus J. Kennedy, in *La Revue des Langues Romanes*, 92 (1988), 253–264.

Le Ditié de Jehanne d'Arc, eds. Angus J. Kennedy and Kenneth Varty (Oxford, 1977).

Le Débat sur le Roman de la Rose, ed. Eric Hicks (Paris, 1977).

The Epistle of the Prison of Human Life with an Epistle to the Queen of France and Lament on the Evils of the Civil War, ed. Josette Wisman (New York, 1984).

Epistre de la prison de vie humaine, ed. Angus J. Kennedy (Glasgow, 1984).

La Lamentacion sur les maux de la France. In *Mélanges de langue et littérature françaises du Moyen Age et de la Renaissance offerts à Charles Foulon*, ed. Angus J. Kennedy (Rennes, 1980), 177–185.

Lettre a Isabeau de Baviere. In *Anglo-Norman Letters and Petitions from all Souls Ms. 182*, ed. M. Dominica Legge (Oxford, 1971).

Le Livre du Chemin de long estude, ed. Robert Püschel (Berlin, Paris, 1881; new ed. Berlin 1887; rpt of 1887 ed: Geneva, 1974).

Le Livre du Corps de policie, ed. Robert H. Lucas (Geneva, 1967).

Le Livre des fais et bonnes meurs du sage Roy Charles V. Ed. Suzanne Solente, 2 vols. (Paris, 1936–1940).

Le Livre de la Mutacion de fortune, ed. Suzanne Solente. 4 vols. (Paris, 1959–1966).

Le Livre de la paix, ed. Charity Cannon Willard (The Hague, 1958).

Oeuvres poétiques de Christine de Pisan, ed. Maurice Roy. 3 vols. (Paris, 1886–1896).

Poems of Cupid, God of Love: Christine de Pizan's "Epistre au dieu d'Amours" and "Dit de la Rose"; Thomas Hoccleve's "The Letter of Cupid"; with George Sewell's "The Proclamation of Cupid," eds. and trs. Thelma S. Fenster, Mary Carpenter Erler (Leiden, 1990).

Sept Psaumes Allegorisés, ed. Ruth Ringland Rains (Washington, D.C., 1956).

4. STUDIES OF OR RELATED TO *THE BOOK OF THE DUKE OF TRUE LOVERS*

Bagoly, Suzanne. "Christine de Pizan et l'art de 'dictier' ballades." *Le Moyen Age*, 92 (1986), 41–67.

Cerquiglini, Jacqueline. Introduction to *Cent ballades d'amant et de dame* (Paris, 1982), 7–24.

Dow, Blanche Hinman. *The Varying Attitude toward Women in French Literature of the 15th Century*. Vol. 1 (New York, 1936), esp. 236–241, 256.

Dulac, Liliane. "Christine de Pisan et le malheur des *vrais amans*," in *Mélanges de langue et littérature offerts à Pierre Le Gentil* (Paris, 1973), 223–33.

Kemp-Welch, Alice. *Of Six Medieval Women* (London, 1913; rpt. Williamstown, MA, 1972), esp. 131–133.

Le Gentil, Pierre. "Christine de Pisan, poète méconnu." In *Mélanges d'histoire littéraire offerts à Daniel Mornet* (Paris, 1951), 1–10.

Painter, Sidney. *French Chivalry* (Baltimore, 1940), esp. 29, 117, 133, 147.

Riesch, Helene. *Frauengeist der Vergangenheit: Biographisch-literarische Studien* (Freiburg, 1915).

Willard, Charity Cannon. "Christine de Pizan's *Cent Ballades d'Amant et de Dame:* Criticism of Courtly Love." In *Court and Poet: Selected Proceedings of the Third Congress of the International Courtly Literature Society (Liverpool 1980)*, ed. Glyn S. Burgess. Arca Classical and Medieval Texts, Paper and Monographs, 5. (Liverpool, 1981), 357–364.

——. "Concepts of Love according to Guillaume de Machaut, Christine de Pizan and Pietro Bembo." In *The Spirit of the Court. Selected Proceedings of the Fourth Congress of the International Courtly Literature Society (Toronto 1983)*, eds. Glyn S. Burgess, Robert A. Taylor (Cambridge, 1985), 386–392.

——. "Lovers' Dialogues in Christine de Pizan's Lyric Poetry from the *Cent Ballades* to the *Cent Ballades d'Amant et de Dame.*" *Fifteenth-Century Studies*, 4 (1981), 167–180.

Wolfzettel, Friedrich. "Zur Poetik der Subjektivität bei Christine de Pisan." In *Lyrik des ausgehenden 14 und 15 Jahrhunderts*, ed. Franz V. Spechtler (Amsterdam, 1984), 379–397.

5. BIOGRAPHICAL STUDIES

Du Castel, Françoise. *Damoiselle Christine de Pizan, veuve de M. Etienne de Castel* (Paris, 1972).

——. *Ma Grand-mère Christine de Pizan* (Paris, 1936).

Favier, Margerite. *Christine de Pisan: Muse des cours souveraines* (Lausanne, 1967).

McLeod, Enid. *The Order of the Rose. The Life and Ideals of Christine de Pizan* (London, 1976).

Moulin, Jeanne. *Christine de Pisan* (Paris, 1962).

Nys, Ernest. *Christine de Pisan et ses principales oeuvres* (Brussels, 1914).

Pernoud, Regine. *Christine de Pisan* (Paris, 1982).

Pinet, Marie-Josèphe. *Christine de Pisan (1364–1430). Etude biographique et littéraire* (Paris, 1982).

Solente, Suzanne. "Christine de Pisan." *Histoire littéraire de la France*. Vol. 40 (Paris, 1969), 335–422.

Willard, Charity Cannon. *Christine de Pizan: Her Life and Works* (New York, 1984).

6. LITERARY STUDIES

Badel, Pierre-Yves. *Le Roman de la Rose au XIVe siècle* (Geneva, 1980).

Bell, Susan G. "Christine de Pizan (1364–1430): Humanism and the Problem of a Studious Woman." *Feminist Studies,* 3 (1976), 173–184.

Bornstein, Diane. "The Ideal of the Lady of the Manor as Reflected in Christine de Pizan's *Livre des Trois Vertus,*" in Bornstein, 117–128.

——, ed. *Ideals for Women in the Works of Christine de Pizan* (Kalamazoo, MI, 1981).

Brownlee, Kevin. "Discourses of the Self: Christine de Pizan and the *Rose.*" *Romanic Review* 78 (1988), 199–221.

——. "Generic Hybrids." In *A New History of French Literature,* 88–93.

——. "Structures of Authority in Christine de Pizan's *Ditié de Jehanne d'Arc.*" In *Discourses of Authority in Medieval and Renaissance Literature,* eds. Kevin Brownlee, Walter Stephens, (Hanover, NH, and London), 1989, 131–50.

Bumgardner, George. "Tradition and Modernity from 1380 to 1405: Christine de Pizan." Diss. Yale, 1970.

Cerquiglini, Jacqueline. "Trials of Eros," in *A New History of French Literature,* 114–118.

Combettes, Bernard. "Une notion stylistique et ses rapports avec la syntaxe. Narration et description chez Christine de Pizan." In *Le Génie de la forme. Mélanges de langue et littérature offerts à Jean Mourot.* XV (Nancy, 1982), 51–58.

Cropp, Glynnis. "Boèce et Christine de Pizan." *Le Moyen Age,* 87 (1981), 387–417.

Delany, Sheila. "Rewriting Woman Good. Gender and the Anxiety of Influence in Two Medieval Texts." In *Chaucer in the Eighties,* eds. J.N. Wasserman, R.J. Blanch (Syracuse, NY, 1986), 75–92.

Dulac, Liliane, "Inspiration mystique et savoir politique: les conseils aux veuves chez Francesco da Barbarino et chez Christine de Pizan," in *Mélanges à la Mémoire de Franco Simone* (Geneva, 1980), 113–141.

——. "*Le Livre du dit de Poissy* de Christine de Pizan: Poème éclaté ou montage signifiant." In *Ecrire pour dire. Etudes sur le dit médiéval.* Bernard Ribemont, ed. (Paris, 1990), 9–28.

Fenster, Thelma. "Did Christine Have a Sense of Humor? The Evidence of the *Epistre au dieu d'Amours.*" In Richards et al.

Ferrante, Joan. "Public Postures and Private Maneuvers: Roles Medieval Women Play." In *Women and Power in the Middle Ages,* 213–229.

Finkel, Helen. "The Portrait of the Woman in the Works of Christine de Pisan," *Les Bonnes Feuilles,* 3, no. 2 (1974), 138–151.

Hindman, Sandra L. *Christine de Pizan's "Epistre d'Othea." Painting and Politics at the Court of Charles VI* (Toronto, 1988).

Hicks, Eric. Introduction to *Le Débat du Roman de la Rose,* ix–liv. See Recent Modern Editions.

Hult, David F. "Jean de Meun's Continuation of *Le roman de la rose,*" in *A New History of French Literature,* 97–103.

Huot, Sylvia. "Seduction and Sublimation: Christine de Pizan, Jean de Meun, and Dante." *Romance Notes,* 25 (1985), 361–373.

Kelly, Douglas. "Reflections on the Role of Christine de Pizan as a Feminist Writer." *Sub-stance*, 2 (1972), 63–71.

Kelly, Joan. "Early Feminist Theory and the Querelle des Femmes, 1400–1789." *Signs*, 8 (1982), 4–28. Rpt. in *Women, History and Theory* (Chicago, 1984).

Laidlaw, James C. "Christine de Pizan—A Publisher's Progress." *Modern Language Review*, 82 (1987), 35–75.

——. "Christine de Pizan—An Author's Progress." *Modern Language Review*, 78 (1983), 532–50.

Laigle, Mathilde. *Le Livre des Trois Vertus de Christine de Pisan et son milieu historique et littéraire* (Paris, 1912).

Margolis, Nadia. "The Poetics of History in Christine de Pizan's *Mutacion de Fortune*." Diss. Stanford, 1977.

——. "The Poetess as Historian." *Journal of the History of Ideas*, 47 (1986), 361–375.

——. "Elegant Closures: The Use of the Diminutive in Christine de Pizan and Jean de Meun." In Richards et al.

A New History of French Literature, ed. Denis Hollier (Cambridge, Mass., 1989).

Noakes, Susan. "From Boccaccio to Christine de Pizan." In *Timely Reading, Between Exegesis and Interpretation*. (Ithaca, NY, 1988), 98–134.

Paradis, Françoise. "Une polyphonie narrative: pour une description de la structure des *Cent ballades d'amant et de dame* de Christine de Pizan," *Bien dire et bien apprendre*, no. 8 (1991), 127–140.

Phillippy, Patricia A. "Establishing Authority: Boccaccio's *De Claris Mulieribus* and Christine de Pizan's *Le Livre de la Cité des Dames*." *Romanic Review*, 77 (1986), 167–194.

Poirion, Daniel. "Narcisse et Pygmalion dans le *Roman de la Rose*." In *Essays in Honor of Louis Francis Solano*, eds. Raymond Cormier, Urban T. Holmes. Studies in the Romance Languages and Literatures, 92 (Chapel Hill, NC, 1970), 153–165.

——. *Le Poète et le Prince: l'Evolution du lyrisme courtois de Guillaume de Machaut à Charles d'Orléans*. (Paris, 1965).

——. *Littérature française. Le Moyen Age II—1300–1480*. (Paris, 1971).

Price, Paola Malpezzi. "Masculine and Feminine Personae in the Love Poetry of Christine de Pisan," *Women and Literature*, 1 (1980), 37–53.

Reno, Christine. "Christine de Pizan: Feminism and Irony." In Jonathan Beck and Gianni Mombello, eds., *Seconda Miscellanea di Studi e Ricerche sul Quattrocento francese. Etudes réunies par F. Simone* (Chambéry-Turin, 1981), 127–33.

——. "Virginity as an Ideal in Christine de Pizan's *Cité des Dames*." In Bornstein, 69–90.

——. "Feminist Aspects of Christine de Pizan's "Epistre d'Othea a Hector." *Studi Francesi*, 71 (1980), 271–276.

Richards, Earl Jeffrey. "Christine de Pizan and the Question of Feminist Rhetoric," *Teaching Language through Literature*, 22 (1983), 15–24.

——, ed., with J.B. Williamson, N. Margolis, C. Reno, *Reinterpreting Christine de Pizan: Essays in Honor of Charity Cannon Willard* (Athens, GA, 1991).

Richardson, Lula McDowell. *The Forerunners of Feminism in French Literature of the Renaissance: Part I, From Christine de Pisan to Marie de Gournay* (Baltimore, 1929).

Rigaud, Rose. "Les Idées féministes de Christine de Pisan." Diss. Neuchâtel, 1911.

Schibanoff, Susan. "Taking the Gold out of Egypt: The Art of Reading as a Woman." In

Gender and Reading, Essays on Readers, Texts, and Contexts, eds. E. Flynn and P. Schweickart (Baltimore, London, 1986), 83–106.

Tuve, Rosemund. *Allegorical Imagery: Some Medieval Books and their Posterity* (Princeton, 1966).

Walters, Lori. "The Woman Writer and Literary History: Christine de Pizan's Redefinition of the Poetic *Translatio* in the *Epistre au dieu d'Amours.*" *French Literature Series*, 16 (1989), 1–16.

——. "Fathers and Daughters: Christine de Pizan as Reader of Male Chivalric Orders and Traditions of *Clergie* in the *Dit de la Rose.*" In Richards et al.

Willard, Charity Cannon. "A Fifteenth-Century View of Women's Role in Medieval Society: Christine de Pizan's *Livre des Trois Vertus,*" in *The Role of Women in the Middle Ages,* ed. Rosmarie T. Morewedge (Albany, NY, London, 1975), 90–120.

——. "Christine de Pizan's *Livre des Trois Vertus:* Feminine Ideal or Practical Advice?" In Bornstein, 91–116.

——. "A Re-examination of *Le Debat des deux amans.*" *Les Bonnes Feuilles,* 3 (1974), 73–88.

Wisman, Josette. "L'Humanisme dans l'oeuvre de Christine de Pisan." Diss. Catholic Univ. of America, 1976.

7. FURTHER READING ON RELATED SUBJECTS

Reference

Dictionary of Medieval Knighthood and Chivalry: Concepts and Terms. Bradford Broughton, ed. (New York, 1988).

Dictionary of Medieval Knighthood and Chivalry: People, Places, and Events. Bradford Broughton, ed. (New York, 1988).

Dictionary of the Middle Ages. Vols. 1–8, ed. Joseph Strayer; Vol. 9, eds. Collet's Holdings Ltd. Staff (London, 1982–1987).

General and Historical

Artz, Frederick B. *The Mind of the Middle Ages* (New York, 1953).

Autrand, Françoise. *Charles VI. La Folie du roi* (Paris, 1986).

Barber, Richard. *The Knight and Chivalry* (New York, 1974).

Commeaux, Charles. *La Vie quotidienne en Bourgogne au temps des ducs Valois 1364–1477* (Paris, 1979).

Contamine, Philippe. *La Vie quotidienne pendant la Guerre de Cent Ans* (Paris, 1976).

Combes, A. *Jean de Montreuil et le chancelier Gerson. Contribution à l'histoire des rapports de l'humanisme et la théologie en France au début du XVe siècle* (Paris, 1942).

Coville, A. *Gontier et Pierre Col et l'humanisme en France au temps de Charles VI* (Paris, 1934).

Elias, Norbert. *The Court Society,* tr. Edmund Jephcott (Oxford, 1983; rpt. New York).

Favier, Jean. *La Guerre de Cent Ans. 1337–1453* (Paris, 1980).

Froissart, Jean. *Chronicles,* tr. Geoffrey Brereton (Harmondsworth, Middlesex, 1968).

Gies, Frances and Joseph. *Life in a Medieval Castle* (New York, 1974).

Heer, Frederick. *The Medieval World* (London, 1961).

Huizinga, Johan. *The Waning of the Middle Ages.: A Study of the Forms of Life, Thought and Art in France and The Netherlands in the XIVth and XVth Centuries.* Tr. from Dutch (New York, 1949).

Huot, Sylvia. *From Song to Book: The Poetics of Writing in Old French Lyric and Lyrical Narrative Poetry* (Ithaca, NY, 1987).

Jaeger, C. Stephen. *The Origins of Courtliness: Civilizing Trends and the Formation of Courtly Ideals (939–1210)* (Philadelphia, 1985).

Journal d'un Bourgeois de Paris de 1405 à 1449, ed. Colette Beaune (Paris, 1990).

Keen, Maurice. *Chivalry.* (New Haven, CT, 1984).

La Chronique du Religieux de Saint-Denis, contenant le règne de Charles VI de 1380–1422. 6 vols. Ed. L.F. Bellaguet (Paris, 1839–1852).

Labarge, Margaret. *A Small Sound of the Trumpet: Women in Medieval Life* (Boston, 1986).

Maclean, Ian. *The Renaissance Notion of Woman: A Study in the Fortunes of Scholasticism and Medical Science in European Intellectual Life.* Cambridge Monographs on the History of Medicine (Cambridge, 1980).

Markale, Jean. *Isabeau de Bavière* (Paris, 1982).

Ouy, Gilbert. "Paris l'un des principaux foyers de l'humanisme en Europe au début du XVe siècle." *Bulletin de l'Histoire de Paris et de l'Ile de France,* 1967–68 [1970], 71–98.

Paston Letters and Papers of the Fifteenth Century, ed. N. Davis (Oxford, 1971).

Pernoud, Régine. *La Femme au temps des cathédrales* (Paris, 1980).

Perroy, Edouard. *La Guerre de Cent ans* (Paris, 1945).

Seward, Desmond. *The Hundred Years' War. The English in France, 1337–1453* (New York, 1978).

Simone, Franco. *Il Rinascimento francese* (Turin, 1961). English translation by H. Gaston Hall (New York, 1969).

Thibault, Marcel. *Isabeau de Bavière, reine de France. La Jeunesse 1370–1405* (Paris, 1903).

Verdon, Jean. *Isabeau de Bavière* (Paris, 1981).

Women and Power in the Middle Ages, eds. Mary Erler, Maryanne Kowaleski (Athens, GA, 1988).

Women in Medieval Society, ed. Susan Mosher Stuard (Philadelphia, 1976).

Women in the Medieval World, eds. Julius Kirshner and Suzanne Wemple (New York, 1985).

Literature and Literary Studies

Andreas Capellanus. *The Art of Courtly Love,* tr. and ed. J.J. Parry (New York, 1964).

Dante. *The Banquet,* tr. Christopher Ryan (Stanford, 1989).

Froissart, Jean. *Oeuvres,* ed. Kervyn de Lettenhove (Brussels, 1866).

Jordan, Constance. *Renaissance Feminism. Literary Texts and Political Models* (Ithaca, NY, 1990).

Patch, Howard Rollin. *The Tradition of Boethius; a Study of His Importance in Medieval Culture* (New York, 1935).

Daniel Poirion, *Le Roman de la Rose* (Paris, 1973).

Poèmes d'Alain Chartier, ed. James Laidlaw (Paris, 1988).

The Poetical Works of Alain Chartier, ed. James Laidlaw (Cambridge, 1974).

Le Roman de la Rose, ed. Daniel Poirion (Paris, 1974).

The Romance of the Rose, tr. Charles Dahlberg (Hanover, NH, 1971).

The Romance of the Rose, tr. Harry Robbins (New York, 1962).

Tournaments and Amusements

Barber, Richard, and Juliet Barker, *Tournaments. Jousts, Chivalry and Pageants in the Middle Ages*. (Woodbridge, Suffolk; New York, 1989).

Barker, Juliet R.V. *The Tournament in England 1100–1400*. (Woodbridge, Suffolk; Wolfeboro, NH, 1986).

Clephan, R. Coltman. *The Tournament, Its Periods and Phases* (1919). Rpt. New York: Ungar, 1967).

Cripps-Day, Francis Henry. *The History of the Tournament in England and France* (Bernard Quaritch, 1918).

Dolmetsch, Mabel. *Dances of England and France from 1450 to 1600 with their Music and Authentic Manner of Performance* (New York, 1975).

Costume

Brooks, Iris. *Western European Costume: Thirteenth to Seventeenth Century*, 2 vols. (London, 1939).

Evans, Joan. *Dress in Mediaeval France* (Oxford, 1952).

Newton, Stella Mary. *Fashion in the Age of the Black Prince. A Study of the Years 1340–1365* (Woodbridge, Suffolk; Totowa, NJ, 1980).

Scott, Margaret, *Late Gothic Europe, 1400–1500*. The History of Dress Series (London, 1980).

Staniland, Kay. "The Medieval 'Corset'." *Costume. The Journal of the Costume Society*, 3 (1969), 10–13.

Yarwood, Doreen. *European Costume. 4000 Years of Fashion* (London, 1975).